As he leaned over cabin, looking do doors snapped open behind him and Rafe jumped, swinging around.

Dr. Mel Murphy was clad in a pair of slim-fitting jeans and a no-nonsense pair of walking boots. The strap of a zipped nylon bag was looped across her body, and if he wasn't very much mistaken, it was a traveling medical kit. The sight of his own larger backpack didn't seem to deter her, and she closed and locked the doors.

"Ready?" When she looked up at him, he noticed that her eyes were a more compelling blue than in the photographs, more like the water swirling beneath them. Suddenly Rafe felt unsteady, as if they too had the power to sweep him off his feet.

Not a good idea when there was a storm coming. Not a good idea period.

"Yep. This way." He started to walk back to the beach, hearing her footsteps behind him.

You could turn your back on a fire and still feel its heat. And, despite her quiet, well-measured facade, Dr. Murphy did have a touch of fire about her.

Dear Reader,

I've long wanted to write a story where my hero and heroine are stranded on an idyllic tropical island! Although for this book, Rafe and Mel have to shoulder the responsibility of being the only doctors on the island when a tropical storm hits.

Maybe that's not such a bad thing. Some holiday romances can't withstand the onslaught of getting back to reality, but Mel and Rafe have no chance to relax—they're dealing with all of the issues and problems they confront in their everyday lives.

Which brings me to something else I've been reminded of recently. A sudden illness in the family left me struggling to find time to write, but when I did, it was even more of a joy. There's something about a romance that gives us all a few hours' holiday from our everyday lives and allows us to return refreshed and reinvigorated.

I hope you enjoy reading Mel and Rafe's story!

Annie x

STRANDED WITH THE ISLAND DOCTOR

ANNIE CLAYDON

HARLEQUIN
MEDICAL
ROMANCE

If you purchased this book without a cover you should be aware that this book is stolen property. It was reported as "unsold and destroyed" to the publisher, and neither the author nor the publisher has received any payment for this "stripped book."

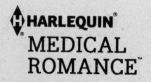

HARLEQUIN®
MEDICAL ROMANCE™

Recycling programs for this product may not exist in your area.

ISBN-13: 978-1-335-73729-8

Stranded with the Island Doctor

Copyright © 2022 by Annie Claydon

All rights reserved. No part of this book may be used or reproduced in any manner whatsoever without written permission except in the case of brief quotations embodied in critical articles and reviews.

This is a work of fiction. Names, characters, places and incidents are either the product of the author's imagination or are used fictitiously. Any resemblance to actual persons, living or dead, businesses, companies, events or locales is entirely coincidental.

For questions and comments about the quality of this book, please contact us at CustomerService@Harlequin.com.

Harlequin Enterprises ULC
22 Adelaide St. West, 41st Floor
Toronto, Ontario M5H 4E3, Canada
www.Harlequin.com

Printed in U.S.A.

Cursed with a poor sense of direction and a propensity to read, **Annie Claydon** spent much of her childhood lost in books. A degree in English literature followed by a career in computing didn't lead directly to her perfect job—writing romance for Harlequin—but she has no regrets in taking the scenic route. She lives in London: a city where getting lost can be a joy.

Books by Annie Claydon

Harlequin Medical Romance

Dolphin Cove Vets

Healing the Vet's Heart

London Heroes

Falling for Her Italian Billionaire
Second Chance with the Single Mom

Winning the Surgeon's Heart
A Rival to Steal Her Heart
The Best Man and the Bridesmaid
Greek Island Fling to Forever
Falling for the Brooding Doc
The Doctor's Reunion to Remember
Risking It All for a Second Chance
From the Night Shift to Forever

Visit the Author Profile page
at Harlequin.com for more titles.

With grateful appreciation for friends in a crisis

**Praise for
Annie Claydon**

"A spellbinding contemporary medical romance
that will keep readers riveted to the page,
Festive Fling with the Single Dad is a highly
enjoyable treat from Annie Claydon's immensely
talented pen."

—*Goodreads*

CHAPTER ONE

Dr Mel Murphy liked to keep busy. She wouldn't even have been on this holiday if it weren't for her daughter Amy and new son-in-law, who had gifted it to her as a thank-you for helping organise their wedding, and 'keeping us sane'. The thank-you was unnecessary, but the thought that her daughter had grown into the kind of person who would think to do such a thing was immeasurably precious.

She'd arrived on Nadulu Island, in the Maldives, on Saturday, and been shown to one of the small, luxurious cabins that were suspended over the clear blue water like a string of pearls. The view was magnificent, the movement of the sea beneath her calming. Mel had unpacked and decided to go for a walk.

White sand and tall palm trees encircled the island, and it had taken just over an hour to arrive back where she'd started. She'd gone to the hotel bar, ordered a many-coloured cocktail and made the acquaintance of a few of the other guests staying here.

Everything was calm and tranquil, from the lapping of the waves to the smiles and unhurried pace of the island. Maybe Amy had been right and everyone needed a break, even from the most carefully balanced and rewarding of lives. Mel could almost feel herself winding down and although she had the nagging feeling that she must have missed *something* that needed to be done, she was reconciling herself to letting everything beyond the sapphire-blue of the sea get along without her for three weeks.

This island of calm had seemed like an impossible goal for much of her life. Mel had battled the crippling anxiety that had followed in the wake of her relationship with Amy's father, like the wash of one of the speedboats on the horizon. When Michael had left, a week before Amy's first birthday, it had seemed that there was no future at all beyond the next ten minutes. But her family had picked her back up again, and slowly Mel's horizons had begun to widen. Her parents had looked after Amy while Mel went back to university to finish her medical degree. Over the years the dreams that she'd thought were gone for ever, standing on her own two feet and making a career and a good home for her daughter, had gradually materialised.

She'd done it all for Amy, in the belief that one of the best things she could pass down to her was a good example, and now everything was changing again. Her precious girl was grown, with a husband, a career and a home of her own. Mel had planned for this, just as she planned for everything. Those carefully laid building blocks, the four days a week spent travelling into the heart of London to work as a consultant neurologist, then three days involved with the village community where she lived and her favourite local medical charity, would sustain her. They'd help protect Mel from the anxiety that had plagued her for so many years after Michael had left, his last unwanted gift to her.

She took the wooden walkway out across the water and back to her cabin, to read until her drooping eyelids told her it was time for an early night. The hotel's brochure promised a busy activities programme, and maybe she'd try one of the water sports on offer tomorrow...

The morning dawned bright and clear, she supposed much like most other mornings here. Breakfast was ordered, delivered and eaten, and Mel made sure that the bag slung across her body contained enough sunscreen. A pair of Bermuda shorts and a cotton top would be suitable for any adventure that presented itself this morning.

As she closed the sliding doors of her cabin, one of the hotel staff came hurrying along the walkway, knocking at each of the sliding glass doors and waiting to deliver a message. As a nod to the unhurried pace of the island, Mel didn't walk towards her to see what was going on, but waited, taking in the scent of the warm sea.

'The manager, Mr Manike, has asked that all guests come to the reception area, for a meeting which is to be held in the main restaurant. Thank you.'

Since there seemed to be no alternative on offer Mel smiled. She supposed that it didn't really matter what the meeting was about, she had all day and nowhere in particular to be.

'Okay. Thanks, I'm on my way.'

The hotel entrance was surprisingly busy, people standing in groups and talking to each other, the hotel staff moving amongst them. The young man behind the reception desk seemed inundated with enquiries and had a queue to deal with. The laissez-faire atmosphere of the place seemed to be slipping and Mel caught the attention of a young woman, clad in the hotel's uniform.

'What's going on?'

The woman smiled. 'Everything's all right.'

Not what she'd asked, although it was nice to know. But something prickled at the back of Mel's neck. As a doctor, she was well aware of the fact that *everything's all right* generally meant that there was a suspicion that something might not be.

'So…' How to phrase this? 'What's everyone doing here?'

Another smile. 'We've had news that there is some heavy rain in the area. It's not a problem, ma'am, the hotel is fully equipped to deal with such things. It may miss us altogether.'

Heavy rain didn't sound like anything to panic about, even if the pictures in the hotel brochure did imply that the skies would be unremittingly cloudless for the duration of one's visit. She'd heard that rainstorms here weren't uncommon, and the hotel must be able to deal with them as a matter of course. Mel wondered exactly what level of rain was needed to provoke the kind of bustle that she was seeing around her.

'You mean a hurricane?'

The woman laughed nervously. 'Oh, no, ma'am, we don't get hurricanes in this area. Just rain.'

Maybe Mel should go halves with her and assume a tropical storm. But the woman's attention had been caught by one of her colleagues, who had called to her and beckoned her over, and there was no chance to ask. The hotel guests were being shepherded into the large dining area, open to the sea on one side, where seats had been laid out in neat rows rather than informally grouped. Mel wondered if this might be an opportunity to gather a little more information, gravitating towards two women who were sitting alone together.

'Is this seat taken?'

'No.' The woman who answered her looked to be in her mid-thirties, and her tan showed that she'd been here for longer than just a day. 'It's terrible, isn't it?'

Out of habit, her most reassuring smile sprang to Mel's lips. 'I don't really know what's happening. One of the concierges says rain.'

'I'm sure that's underplaying things. There's going to be a big storm, we heard about it this morning.' The two women nodded conspiratorially, obviously privy to a little local knowledge. 'It's going to spoil our holiday.'

'And we're in one of the cabins, out on the water.' Her companion looked as if she was about to burst into tears. 'Even here in the main building…those palm trees don't look at all safe, do they?'

Mel considered the palm trees, waving gently in the breeze outside. They were huge, probably here long before the hotel had been built. She'd have to consult the internet, but common sense told her that if they'd survived any length of time on the island then they had a natural advantage in the face of storms.

'They seem quite flexible. Isn't it the more rigid type of tree that generally comes down during a storm?'

Her answer didn't quell the anxiety that Mel was trying very hard not to think about. Nor did it appear to console the woman, who looked as if she was about to burst into tears. Mel shot her a reassuring smile as Mr Manike stepped out in front of them, and every head turned towards him.

'Ladies and gentlemen.' His soft-spoken tones were amplified by a microphone. 'I will update you on exactly what is happening. We have received a warning of rain and winds of up to gale force eight which are approaching us. If the storm maintains its current course then it will be with us at some time during the afternoon.'

A murmur ran around the assembled guests. Mel tried to recall the late-night weather report on the radio, back in England, and whether gale force eight was anything to worry about.

'There is nothing to worry about.' Mr Manike appeared to have anticipated the question before anyone got the chance to ask. 'We will move all of the guests who are staying in the water cabins, to spend the night in the hotel building, purely as a precautionary measure. I can assure you that we will be quite safe, the hotel has been built to withstand any kind of weather and we are currently putting the storm shutters in place. We will have a safe and pleasant evening.'

There was a barrage of shouted questions and Mr Manike appealed for quiet, saying that he would answer everyone's concerns. Hands shot up, and one by one he addressed the questions. No, there was no possibility of evacuating onto the mainland, it was a lot safer to stay here. Yes, everyone from the cabins would be given first class rooms in the hotel building and no one would be asked to share. Yes, the storm was expected to pass and everyone could resume their holidays. No, he couldn't say exactly when.

This was just the kind of thing that was prone to make her feel anxious, vague risks coupled with equally vague reassurances. Maybe this was payback time for having thought that all the world's problems would just drift past her, carried away by the tide…

Mel straightened herself, trying to concentrate on coping mechanisms. This wasn't her fault, and no amount of thinking about it was going to change the weather. There were people here on the island who could deal with this much better than she could, and she should let them get on with it. She still couldn't help wishing that someone would give her a clear and concise explanation of the situation and something to do…

Or… Something to take her mind off the thousand different scenarios that were beginning to jostle in her head. Suddenly, as if in answer to an unspoken prayer, one of the double doors into the restaurant flipped open and someone walked in.

At last! This man had an unmistakable air of action and purpose about him. A magnetism that would have made Mel shiver in any situation, but right now it had the added bonus of driving every other thought from her head. Tanned and a little lined, his dark curly hair showing a few streaks of white, he had the look of someone whose experience was something that any woman would be glad to be on the receiving end of. He wore a canvas jacket and heavy boots, as if he were about to cut his way through a jungle.

You Tarzan, me Jane.

Maybe not the kind of guy you'd want to indulge in a long conversation with, the way he walked was a little too swaggering. Very nice to look at though, even if touching was probably not a good idea, and he was ideal for taking her mind off things for the next ten minutes.

The manager caught sight of him and beckoned him over, temporarily ignoring the next shouted question. There was a click as the microphone was muted and the two spoke briefly, nodding in agreement about something.

'Is there anyone here with medical training? I understand that a Dr Murphy is a guest at the hotel…' Tarzan had a cut-glass English accent and was smiling now. Before Mel had properly admitted to herself that it was a nice smile, she was on her feet.

'I'm Dr Murphy.' She bit her lip before she could admit that her name *wasn't* Jane.

'Great. This way…' Tarzan turned, making for the exit without looking back at her. A man of the jungle who was clearly used to having his every word obeyed by the creatures around him. Mel threaded her way past the line of seated guests and found that he was holding the door open for her.

'Has someone been hurt?' The manager had gone back to answering questions and Mel stopped in the doorway, blocking his path. If someone *had* been hurt then it would be a little more appropriate to just tell her what was going on and allow her to lead the way.

Tarzan gave a quick shake of his head, gesturing her through the door and closing it behind them. 'No, I'm here to see the wife of a member of staff. She's in perfect health, but she *is* pregnant and her due date is today. I'm going to have to decide how best to provide her with medical care over the next twenty-four hours.'

Was there really such a thing as a come-to-bed voice, or was a sudden appreciation of his scent and the look in his dark eyes messing with her head? It was a bit more to the point to ask why he assumed that *he* was qualified to make medical decisions.

'I'm a neurologist, but I have ten years' experience of working with a childbirth trust and I've delivered many babies during that time.' Mel folded her arms, waiting for him to acknowledge that leaving any decisions to her might be a good idea.

His brow creased slightly, as if that came as a surprise. 'Your internet profile didn't mention anything about a childbirth trust...'

'That's because I generally keep my work separate from my personal interests.' Mel rattled off the web address for the Trust. 'It's good to know that you took the time to look me up. Are you going to return the favour and tell me who *you* are?'

That grin of his was straight off a cinema

screen. Mel reminded herself that cinema screens weren't real life.

'Rafe Davenport. I'm temporarily the doctor for this area. I'm not sure what the web says about me...'

He might have mentioned that he too was a doctor but he'd clearly been too busy taking charge. Mel resisted the temptation to take her phone from her bag and do an internet search, right then and there.

'I'm sure I can manage to find you. You're based here on the island?'

'No, I flew in this morning. I know you're supposed to be on holiday, but any help you feel able to give would be appreciated.'

Another thing that Dr Davenport needed reminding of. 'You think that sorry, I'm *on holiday* is an option for any doctor?'

The quick shake of his head told her that it wasn't an option for him, and Mel wished he'd thought to extend her the same courtesy. But even if there had been any choice in the matter, being annoyed by Dr Davenport's extraordinary magnetism seemed a better alternative than sitting around and worrying about things she couldn't do anything to change.

'We have a walk ahead of us. Have you got more suitable shoes? Maybe jeans...?'

Nowhere was all that far to go in this place,

and Mel assumed he was referring to some kind of short cut, through the densely wooded centre of the island. Although, of course, he wasn't going to say *where* they were going, that would be far too much information. Dr Davenport had decided he was in charge and it seemed that he intended to stay that way.

'I have jeans in my cabin.' Mel couldn't resist taking a dig at him. 'Suitable shoes tends to vary, according to where I'm planning to go.'

He grinned again and she raised an eyebrow. Mel hadn't been aware that she was joking.

'We need to get to the other side of the island, and the quickest way is through those trees.' He gestured towards the thickly wooded area that occupied the centre of the island 'I'll go and fetch my things from the plane and see you by the walkway to the cabins.'

He turned, walking purposefully out of the reception area and onto the beach. A small sea plane was moored against the jetty and Mel made for the wooden walkway that led to her cabin. Flipping the lock on the sliding glass doors that led to the living area, she banged them shut again, just in case Dr Davenport thought it was a good idea to join her and pick out the most suitable thing for her to wear for a trek across the island.

* * *

Rafe would admit he probably *had* been a little economical with the details, and that Dr Murphy had been quite right in quizzing him. He put the omissions down to his curious preoccupation with whether her smile would have the same effect on him in person as the electronic version had done. He was still waiting. Dr Murphy clearly hadn't found a great deal to smile about yet.

Before he'd left Male', the capital of the long string of islands that made up the Maldives, he'd spoken with the manager here and learned that a doctor was a guest at the hotel. Keeping Mr Manike on the line, he'd searched the internet and found a Dr Amelia Murphy, a consultant neurologist, practising at a select private hospital in London. He'd described the woman in the photograph in front of him, failing to mention his own reaction to her smile, which was no one's business but his own, and Mr Manike had confirmed that this was the right person.

Rafe had decided to take this good news with a pinch of caution. A doctor was a doctor, everyone had the same basic training. Ideally he would have preferred someone who had some recent experience of childbirth or emergency medicine and, although Dr Murphy was most probably excellent in her own environment, the island didn't have the battalions of support staff and cutting-edge equipment to support her that she'd likely be used to in the private sector. But beggars couldn't be choosers and Rafe was accustomed to making good use of every resource at his disposal.

The smile was the real problem. Or…actually not a problem at all… It was his reaction to it that disturbed Rafe. The way she looked at the camera, quiet assurance in the curve of her perfect lips. He'd always been attracted to women who would present him with challenges, and when he added Dr Murphy's undeniable beauty to the equation he couldn't deny the answering thump of his heart. It was enough to distract any man from the most pressing of missions, and he needed to stay focused. But he also needed her help, and had decided that staying one step ahead of her would avoid any unwelcome interferences.

And… Dr Murphy had put him straight without any trouble at all, which had left him grinning at her like a starry-eyed fool. As he walked to the sea plane, he found himself pulling his phone from his back pocket and typing the web address she'd given him into the browser.

Bad move. The picture of her on the childbirth trust's website was a little more informal, her smile warmer and yet somehow more purposeful. Rafe flipped past it quickly, reading that she was a trustee of the charity and clearly something of a campaigner, advocating for culturally appropriate and individual care for women during their pregnancy. The group pictures that followed left him in no doubt that she based her advice on hands-on involvement.

He resisted the temptation to sit in the cockpit of the plane and take a closer look at the pictures. Dr Murphy might have proved her worth in many different situations but not in the one that faced them right now. Until she did that, he would keep his eye on the goal of keeping everyone safe during the oncoming storm, and Dr Murphy would stay firmly in his rear-view mirrors.

He put his phone back into his pocket and hauled the medical kit from the plane, shouldering it and walking back towards the cabin that he'd seen her disappear into when he'd furtively looked over his shoulder to catch another glimpse of her. The sea was a little higher than usual maybe, lapping a little less gently against the massive posts that supported the cabins, and the warm breeze was a little stiffer than normal. But they had time. He'd contacted the Meteorological Office when he'd got here and although Mr Manike had sensibly told everyone to be ready for the storm this afternoon, it wasn't expected to reach the island until this evening.

As he leant over the rail outside her cabin, looking down at the sea, the sliding doors snapped open behind him and Rafe jumped, swinging round. Dr Murphy was clad in a pair of slim-fitting jeans and a no-nonsense pair of walking boots. The strap of a zipped nylon bag was looped across her body, and if he wasn't very much mistaken it was a travelling medical kit. The sight of his own, larger, backpack didn't seem to deter her and she closed and locked the doors.

'Ready?' When she looked up at him he noticed that her eyes were a more compelling blue than in the photographs, more like the water swirling beneath them. Suddenly Rafe felt unsteady, as if they too had the power to sweep him off his feet.

Not a good idea when there was a storm coming. Not a good idea, full stop.

'Yep. This way.' He started to walk back to the beach, hearing her footsteps behind him.

You could turn your back on a fire, and yet still feel its heat. And, despite her quiet, well measured façade, Dr Murphy did have a touch of fire about her. Her hair was strawberry blonde and he imagined that in her youth it had been as red as the hottest of embers. And her attitude made it very obvious that she stood no nonsense from anyone.

Even the thought of her made his heart thump, the way it had when he had first met his wife. The way that Rafe had thought it never would again when Annu had died. He could tell himself until he was blue in the face that keeping Dr Murphy at arm's length was a simple matter of keeping focused and dealing with a potentially disastrous situation, but that wasn't the whole story. Feeling the intoxicating sensation of attraction for someone he hardly knew carried with it a sense of the overwhelming grief he'd felt when he'd lost Annu.

It was unsettling because he couldn't control it. And because, despite all of the reasons why he shouldn't, he was still looking forward to crossing swords with the beautiful Dr Murphy.

CHAPTER TWO

RAFE'S STRIDE SEEMED to lengthen as he walked up the beach. Mel matched his pace, trying to avoid the indignity of having him turn and wait for her at the line of trees that ran behind the hotel building. He stopped anyway, looking back at the calm sea and the blue sky.

'When is the storm expected to hit us?' It would be nice to have some kind of a timeframe on all of this.

'This evening some time. It could last for a couple of days.'

'The manager said it would be here this afternoon. He didn't say how long it would last but the implication was that it wouldn't be as long as a couple of days.'

He looked down at her as if she were interrupting a serious line of thought with frivolous questions, and Mel felt a tingle of outrage. Michael had done something of the sort, refusing to answer perfectly reasonable questions about where he'd been until the early hours of the morning, until Mel had finally stopped asking. Her judgement had begun to seem flawed and unreasonable, and she'd been reduced to anxious waiting, going through every possible scenario in her head.

She'd had to work hard to leave that behind. And Rafe was going to have to get used to the idea that even though her expertise didn't run to tropical storms she wasn't entirely useless.

'Mr Manike's a sensible man. Get everyone ready ahead of time, and don't panic people with estimates.'

Right. So it was okay to panic *her,* was it? Anyone in her shoes would be a little afraid of the unknown, and Mel's fears were no different to anyone else's. She knew the difference between irrational anxiety and a perfectly normal reaction to the situation you found yourself in.

'And…it's going to be bigger than normal? I heard that heavy rain isn't unusual here, and the hotel seems to be taking a bit of notice of this one.'

Rafe nodded. 'Yeah, this one is probably going to be heavier than usual.'

'But you can't evacuate anyone?' Mel shrugged. 'Some of the people here have been asking about that…'

He raised an eyebrow, giving her a crooked

half-smile. Mel wondered whether that was the way he got everyone to just comply with his instructions—pure smouldering magnetism.

'Where do you want to go?'

'I'm not going anywhere. I just wondered if there *was* anywhere to go.'

'Not really. The storm's moving in a westerly direction so even if we had the resources to take people to Sri Lanka, which we don't, we'd be heading straight towards it. This is one of the safer islands to be on, there's a very wide shelf between the open sea and the beach, which acts to deaden any high waves. And it's pretty much circular.'

He turned, taking the path that led towards the mass of trees in the centre of the island. Mel decided not to ask why circular was better than any other shape. She could look that up on the internet later.

The internet was a wonderful resource, particularly when you were trying to stay one step ahead of someone. While she'd been getting into her jeans and boots, Mel had managed to do a little multi-tasking, propping her phone on the bed and searching for Dr Rafe Davenport.

'So you work out of a hospital in Sri Lanka?'

He shot a delicious glance over his shoulder and kept walking. 'Yeah, Colombo, but I'm not there all that much. I'm part of a team that provides medical support for people in situations like this. When we're not needed in disaster situations we visit rural areas that are hard to get to. Anywhere that medical treatment is needed and there's some obstacle to that.'

Mel would overlook the term *disaster situations*. There was no point in worrying about every possible permutation of that. As far as she could see there were no disasters happening right now. 'You seem to know the island pretty well.'

'I've been here before, on a number of occasions.'

'And you've flown all the way from Colombo this morning?'

Rafe grinned, shaking his head. 'If I'd tried that in a sea plane I'd be swimming by now. They don't have that kind of range. I was in Male' with a group of doctors who are working on a unified disaster plan for the area, and I commandeered a plane and got myself here.'

Of course. The everyday process of just *asking* for a plane probably didn't occur to him. Commandeering sounded far more his style. As the path ahead began to curve gently to the left, Rafe kept walking straight ahead, plunging into the lush undergrowth. Mel pushed through the vegetation behind him, glad of her jeans and boots. In her experience the straightest route wasn't always the best, but Rafe clearly disagreed.

'I looked at the web address you gave me...' His words floated back towards her and Mel ignored the impulse to wonder whether he'd liked what he saw. He didn't have to like her to accept that she knew what she was talking about.

'And...?'

'I'd been wondering whether my patient might prefer a woman doctor.'

So she'd got the job on the basis of her gender. And talking to Rafe's back was beginning to irritate her as well.

'That's for her to say, isn't it? And, in my experience, quite a lot of people prefer a doctor who knows what they're doing.'

He turned suddenly, flashing a smile over his shoulder that made her legs go to jelly. 'Touché, Dr Murphy.'

'Since you know all about me now, probably best to call me Mel.' Maybe his lips wouldn't curve quite so seductively if they had fewer syllables to work with.

'Rafe.' Apparently he didn't mind too much when people answered him back. That was just as well, because Mel answered back.

At the moment she didn't have much breath for answering back. She stopped for a moment, resting her hand on the trunk of an enormous palm, and Rafe gave her a querying look.

'These trees…' Mel had a sudden and irresistible desire to save face. 'They look as if they've been here for a while.'

'You're wondering about whether the ones around the hotel might come down in the storm?'

'It had crossed my mind.'

'Well, you're right, these have been here for a while and weathered quite a few storms. It's interesting…'

He started walking again, launching into a description of how a palm trunk was made of spongy material and not wood, which made it liable to bend instead of break. Threw in a note about taking care not to be caught by the whipping motion of the trunk, just in case she was feeling too reassured by the knowledge, and broke off to slither down an incline, turning and holding his hand out to her. Mel ignored it. If he could make it with the heavy pack he was carrying, then she was sure she could too.

'You know palms are more closely related to grass, corn and rice than to other trees. And they're pretty old. The first palm trees were around when dinosaurs roamed the earth.'

'Good. I like a survivor.'

Rafe nodded. 'Me too.'

This might just be the first thing that they agreed on.

Reaching the sandy beach on the other side of the island was a relief. They walked out of the shaded claustrophobia of the woodlands into a slightly stiffer breeze than had been blowing when they'd entered and it was finally possible to put a little more distance between herself and Rafe. He was heading purposefully towards a group of brick-built bungalows and, as Mel was beginning to expect, there were no explanations.

Rafe stopped to help a woman lift a heavy shutter into place and then continued towards a bungalow on the far edge of the compound. A man was sitting upright in one of the cane chairs on the veranda and sprang to his feet, obviously awaiting their arrival.

'Dr Davenport. I'm glad you could come.'

Those were obviously the words that Rafe lived for. He was the kind of guy who liked to be needed. To be followed and adored... Wait. Mel could see herself following and adoring that broad-shouldered frame as well, if she wasn't careful. And after the night when Michael had substituted coming home late with not coming home at all, she didn't follow *or* adore. She'd devoted herself to her daughter, her work and the small village community where she lived, in that order. She understood the kind of life that fed her, and what could break her.

Almost break her. Michael had broken her, reducing her to a mess of fear and uncertainty, but she was a lot tougher than she'd been back then. Anxiety wasn't something that ever quite left you, but she could deal with it now. Mel hadn't had a panic attack in years.

But Rafe was making her heart beat faster. His steady gaze made her feel flustered and hot, and it was an effort to gather her thoughts. What she needed was a good old-fashioned crisis to give her one overwhelming problem to focus on, rather than a myriad of inconsequential ones.

Careful what you wish for. Mel surveyed the bungalows around her, storm shutters fixed to the doors and windows. The sound of loud complaint, which had been overwhelming at the hotel, might be noticeably absent here, but these people could do without a crisis that might deprive them of their homes. One which might even threaten the life of a mother and her un-born child. Mel silently apologised to the world in general for forgetting that, and joined Rafe on the steps of the covered veranda that ran around the house.

'This is Dr Mel Murphy...' He gestured towards the man who had come to meet them.

'This is Haroon Khaleel. His wife Zeena is going to be having a baby boy any day now and we're here to see that all goes well.'

'Dr Murphy.' Haroon smiled, holding out his hand. 'It's good of you to come. I heard you're here on holiday.'

'It's my pleasure…' Mel shook Haroon's hand and Rafe interrupted.

'Dr Murphy works with a childbirth trust in England, and we're lucky to have her here.' Clearly it was all right to say that *about* her, even if he seemed to have some objection to saying it to her.

'Ah. Indeed.' Haroon beamed at her, ushering her towards the front door, which was the only method of entry into the house that wasn't boarded up.

'Do you need me?' Rafe called after her, and Mel felt her lip curl as she turned towards him.

'I'll be fine. I'd prefer to make my own examination.' Zeena was about to have her very full attention, and Mel would leave nothing to chance. If that was going to annoy Rafe, then it was an added bonus of doing her job well.

'Great… I'll be over there…' Rafe pointed to a group of women who were struggling to fix a large shutter over a pair of patio doors, and Mel resisted the temptation to roll her eyes. Tarzan never missed an opportunity to be helpful, and neither did Rafe Davenport.

A thorough examination showed that Zeena was in the best of health and that the estimate of her due date was accurate. The baby would be coming very soon, probably at much the same time that the storm was expected to hit. Something needed to be done now, to ensure the safety of both mother and baby.

Despite that, the atmosphere around her was calm and unhurried, which gave Mel time to consider all of the things that could go wrong in greater depth. She sat on the veranda, tapping her finger anxiously against the full glass of lemonade on the table beside her, waiting for Rafe to stop what he was doing and come and discuss what they were going to do next.

His jacket was slung over the railings that bounded one of the verandas and the action of a stiff breeze on the thin collarless shirt he wore underneath didn't leave much to the imagination. In the absence of anything else to distract her, it was tempting to allow her imagination to take all it could get, and picture him wet through...

Enough. Mel concentrated on her finger, willing it to stay still. She needed to be a little more assertive and take control of a situation that threatened the lives of both Zeena and her baby. Taking control of Rafe wouldn't be such a bad thing either, even if that did seem a more baffling process.

'Will you be all right here while I go and talk to Dr Davenport?'

'Of course. You will need to make the arrangements.' Zeena smiled lazily towards where Rafe and her husband were working together, helping with the storm shutters on a neighbouring bungalow. She trusted her husband and the community around her to do what was best for her, and Mel felt a sharp pang of envy. Trust was the one thing that had been noticeably missing, along with Amy's father, when Mel had given birth.

Picking up her glass of lemonade, she walked over to Rafe, waiting while he and Haroon manoeuvred a shutter into place. Rafe turned to her, smiling, and walked over to where she stood.

'Ah, thanks.' He took the glass from her hand and drained it. Then he had the audacity to put the empty glass back into her hand. A sudden flash of uncertainty in his eyes, quickly masked, showed Mel that he knew exactly what he'd just done.

And he'd just love it if she made a thing of it, wouldn't he? Mel smiled up at him.

'You're welcome. You want to know the results of my examination?'

'Um… Yes. Please.' For one moment he was at a disadvantage and Mel felt an inappropriate lurch of triumph in her stomach. She handed Rafe the piece of paper that she'd written the results of her examination on.

'This looks good…' He scanned the paper. 'It's consistent with the notes Zeena's usual doctor gave me.'

'And you didn't think to tell me that you'd been briefed on her medical history?' Lemonade was one thing, but the welfare of a patient was quite another.

He gave a shrug. 'You said you didn't need me.'

He'd thought to test her, more likely. That was the kind of thing that happened with experienced doctors and medical students. Mel felt the back of her neck bristle with outrage.

'You didn't say you had Zeena's notes. There's a reason for making notes, and it's called *working together*. You've heard of pooling experience?' She raised one eyebrow.

'Yes, of course.' He didn't seem much chastened by her rebuke and walked over to his backpack, fetching a battered folder full of notes and handing it to Mel. 'Maybe you'd like to review them and add yours.'

That melting smile. The one that was brighter than the morning sunshine and more lulling than the gentle roll of the waves. *That* was the thing that Mel was going to have to be most careful of. The rest she could deal with without too much difficulty.

'Thank you.' She took the folder, tucking it under her arm in a gesture that implied she'd be keeping hold of it. 'As you've seen from my notes, Zeena's baby will be coming at any time now. I'm assuming you've brought medical supplies with you and I'll need you to make them available to me here, as I'll be staying with her from now on.'

Rafe nodded thoughtfully. 'I think it would be best to transfer her over to the hotel.'

Mel looked around her. 'Does Zeena need to make that journey? Everyone here seems pretty organised and ready for the storm.'

'They are, they're used to this kind of thing and the houses are built to withstand storms. But in this situation I think it's better to concentrate our resources in one place. Many of the men are already working over at the hotel, and if Zeena's here then we'll have two locations to cover. That'll probably be impossible once the storm hits.'

In the plethora of shouted questions, no one

back at the hotel had thought to ask how the families of the men working there might be faring.

'So you're thinking of moving Zeena so that we can provide medical services to everyone at the hotel as well.' Mel frowned. Annoyingly, that sounded like a good alternative to her own proposal. 'It sounds logical, even if it is a little unfair.'

Rafe nodded. 'The hotel has an unusually well equipped medical suite which… I probably should have shown it to you before we left.'

'Yes, you probably should.' Mel couldn't resist agreeing with him.

'There are patient beds available in private rooms, and Zeena will be better off there. And we'll be able to cover the hotel as well. It's a win-win situation.'

Mel thought for a moment. Rafe didn't seem to care too much about her feelings, but he was basing his decisions on what was best for everyone. She couldn't fault him in that and it occurred to her that there was a little more to Rafe than met the eye.

'Okay, I agree. Although if anyone at the hotel runs away with the idea that the islanders are seeking refuge there and forgets to thank them for their help, I may have something to say about it.'

He chuckled, the glint in his eyes telling Mel

that she'd said pretty much what he'd hoped she might. Maybe he was thinking that there was a little more to *her* than met the eye as well, and the idea brought a sizzling tingle to her spine.

'That's a very good idea. I may join you.'

CHAPTER THREE

RAFE WATCHED AS Mel walked back to Zeena, sitting down with her on the veranda. He couldn't shake his fascination with Mel. It wasn't like or dislike but an unthinking tug that transcended any opinion he might have of her, and made him crave her presence.

It had made him wary. She was an unknown quantity, not used to working in this environment, and he had to get the measure of her. That measure should be based on cold, hard logic, not something that fell into the same category as a teenage crush.

But he couldn't fault Mel's judgement. She asked questions and came to the right conclusions. She clearly thought that he was testing her, and she wasn't far wrong, but she'd come through those tests with flying colours.

Maybe he should back off for a moment and examine his own motives a little more carefully. Making sure that an unknown doctor was up to the job was one thing, and he didn't regret withholding information until he'd seen what conclusions Mel came to on her own. But using his natural caution to distance himself from his own feelings was quite another thing, however necessary it seemed at the moment.

He'd come to Sri Lanka soon after he'd fully qualified as a doctor, the years of study and practical experience having made him feel a little stuck in one place. And then he'd met Annu. Straight out of medical school in Colombo, she was several years behind him in her training, but if Rafe had felt that he could take his seniority for granted, Annu had shown him differently. She was fiery and confrontational and had made him earn every single piece of the respect that she'd ultimately handed him.

There had been no way he couldn't fall in love with her. Two doctors working together, who stretched each other to their limits. A woman who was as beguiling as she was beautiful. What else was Rafe to do but beg her to marry him?

The thought of the ceremony still brought longing to his heart. Annu had seemed like a queen, in white and gold, and Rafe had been admitted into a family that was as welcoming as it was large. Ten months later, their son Ashok Chandra Davenport had been born.

At first he'd thought that Annu's fatigue was just the sleepless nights, nursing a new baby. Then he'd convinced her to go for some tests, and the cancer had been discovered. All that Rafe had been able to do was to watch, hoping that each new treatment option might be more effective than the last, while his young wife's fire flickered, and finally died.

He had thought he might die of grief too, but he had a son and he needed to survive. Not just survive, but make a good life. Going back to England now was out of the question. Rafe's family consisted of a couple of aunts, who'd taken very little interest in keeping in touch with a busy medical school student when his parents had died in a road accident. Ash's cousins, uncles, aunts and grandparents were involved and for the most part loving relatives and the boy needed his mother's family as much as he did his father. Rafe had stayed, for the love of his son, and then for the love of a country and its people, who had made him their own and given him purpose.

But he'd never found a woman who could replace Annu. In truth, he hadn't really looked, preferring to expend his energies on bringing his son up and a busy medical career, but then Dr Mel Murphy had found him. Mel was very different from his wife in many ways, but the feeling that his heart was going to jump out of his chest was just the same as when he had first met Annu.

He could ignore it. The same way he'd ignored every other woman who'd thought that a young and then not-so-young widower would be looking to replace the wife that he'd lost. He'd had the one true love of his life, and Annu had left him with a son. Once was enough to last a lifetime.

Wasn't it?

Rafe had never questioned the thought, and he wouldn't do so now.

A two-seater beach buggy wasn't the most usual mode of transport for a pregnant woman, but Rafe was used to using whatever was available and Zeena got into the vehicle with a smile. Rafe drove while Zeena's husband walked alongside her, chatting to her. Mel was part of the trail of women and children, who had opted to take the route around the island instead of the shorter path through the centre, because everyone here stuck with the most vulnerable member of the community.

When they arrived at the hotel a few of the men who were working there stopped to wave. Children ran to their fathers, and were hugged and sent back to their mothers again, so that they could be settled into the accommodation that Mr Manike had waiting for them. It may not be as comfortable as their own homes, but it was spacious and afforded shelter from the storm. Rafe led the way to the hotel's medical suite, and Mel followed with Zeena and Haroon.

'Wow! This is…' Mel looked around her as she walked through the small lobby and into a bright, modern consulting room which boasted equipment and supplies to meet almost any medical emergency.

'A bit over the top?' It was obvious what Mel was thinking.

'Yes, actually. Very useful in the circumstances, but definitely over the top.'

Her face was a picture of surprise, and Rafe couldn't help smiling. 'This was one of the conditions that the developers had to meet when they applied to build here: a medical suite that could handle cases from here and neighbouring islands. We're a relatively long way from Male' and the main hospital.'

Mel frowned. 'A medical suite's not much use without a doctor.'

'There's a visiting doctor for the area, but she's in Colombo at the moment, as part of the working party that brought me to Male'. This is her base when she visits this group of islands.'

'And I suppose it's a reassuring picture to put in the brochure?'

She missed nothing. 'I expect so. But the manager's made full use of what he's been given and made sure that the suite is fit for purpose. It's not just a showpiece.' Rafe turned to Zeena, ushering her through the consulting room and into the private corridor beyond, which led to the patients' accommodation, opening the first door he came to.

'Is this okay for you, Zeena? This room's the biggest, but there are three other rooms and since you're our only in-patient you can take your pick.'

'This is very good. Thank you.' Zeena walked into the room and sat down on the bed, beckoning to her husband, who stepped forward and joined her.

'Right then. We'll leave you to get settled, and then you can have some visitors.' Rafe was under no illusions that there would be plenty of visitors. In fact, elbowing his way through the crowd was likely to be his first consideration if Zeena suddenly went into labour.

'I'll see you later.' Mel gave the couple a warm smile and turned, making her way back up the corridor to the consulting room. Rafe followed her, trying very hard not to notice the relaxed grace with which she moved.

A knock sounded and one of the concierges popped his head around the entrance door to the consulting room. 'Dr Murphy. Dr Davenport...' There was some kind of commotion going on behind him, at the entrance to the medical suite, and the man looked back before slipping through the door and closing it firmly.

'The guests have seen your return. There are many questions, and I assume these must be of a medical nature...'

Rafe turned the corners of his mouth down. He wasn't so sure about that. There was something about being a doctor that allowed people to assume that he was also an authority on keeping safe in any emergency. As it happened he knew quite a bit, but Mr Manike was doing that job extremely well.

But, before he could sound a note of caution, Mel had followed the concierge, out of the medical suite. He heard her gasp of surprise as she was surrounded by the knot of talking people who were waiting at the entrance door to the lobby.

The concierge was doing his best to calm everyone down and restore some order, but suddenly Mel was the centre of everyone's attention. Unwittingly, she'd put herself right in the firing line and everyone was raising their voice so they could be heard over everyone else.

She was partly obscured by the mass of people around her, but he saw her raise her hand shakily to her forehead, as if to shield herself from the wall of noise and people. The concierge looked at her questioningly and her impassive silence seemed only to encourage everyone to press closer and speak more loudly.

And she didn't turn. In a situation where she was clearly out of her depth and needed someone to help her, she didn't look back at him. Rafe grudgingly admitted that he wished she had, telling himself that he'd done nothing to deserve the role of Mel's protector, even though all of his instincts were telling him that he wanted it.

A mind trained to observe and diagnose was automatically running through all of the possibilities. Agoraphobia? Panic attack? Or had the tension in the air got to her and played on those fears that anyone thrust into this kind of situation would feel? Now wasn't the time to stand back and try to assess the situation.

'Quiet!' Rafe raised his voice above the hubbub. He saw Mel jump and resisted the impulse to wade into the melee and pull her out.

Everyone stopped talking suddenly and looked at him. Now that he had control, Rafe knew exactly what to do. Panic was the one thing that Mr Manikc had been trying to avoid, because that was the way people got hurt, and a firm hand was needed.

'Form a line, please. Right here, behind this gentleman…' He guided the nearest person to him to one side of the corridor. The man was grinning smugly at being first in the queue and everyone else got behind him, jockeying for position.

Mel had turned towards him, regarding him silently. Her cheeks were a little red and her eyes seemed just a little moist. He couldn't think about that now, and he couldn't show weakness. Right now, not showing weakness was all about asserting his authority and getting everyone to do what he said without stopping to discuss the matter.

'Who is here with a question?' No one seemed obviously ill or injured and the first thing he needed to do was to restore order, so he could find out who *did* need medical assistance.

Almost every hand shot up. There was something to be said for a queue. It seemed to reawaken everyone's memory of the order of a schoolroom. Just one woman, clearly frustrated by her place halfway down the queue, spoke.

'What about the facilities here in the hotel? Shouldn't guests have first priority?'

He saw Mel stiffen suddenly, squaring her drooping shoulders. 'There are more than enough medical resources here if everyone shares. The islanders have relocated so that medical personnel assigned to them are available if needed by hotel guests.'

Great answer. And Mel's indignant fire seemed to have burned off whatever it was that had put her at a loss in this situation. She was still shaking, but she was visibly pulling herself together.

A few people were nodding, and a woman standing next to the one who'd asked the question voiced her opinion that the arrangement was more than fair. That was good to hear, but Rafe didn't want to encourage any discussion about medical priorities because they weren't going to change. He held his hand up for silence.

'I understand that you all have questions, and they'll be dealt with in due course. Is there anyone here with a medical issue that requires attention?' Rafe glanced at the end of the queue. It was the people who couldn't fend for themselves and push to the front that he was most interested in right now.

A woman's hand went up. 'My little boy...' She had a young child with her, who she was holding protectively against her legs. He strode down the line towards them, ushering the woman to one side.

Suddenly Mel was there, at his elbow. 'I'll take them.'

Rafe nodded, jerking his thumb towards the entrance of the medical suite. She got his meaning immediately, guiding the woman and her child into the lobby of the consulting room.

'Any other concerns about current medical issues or medication?' Rafe looked up and down the line.

'I have a question about my medication…' A man gestured to catch his attention.

'So do I.' A woman spoke up and Rafe beckoned towards the concierge.

'Right, I want you both to stand over there, please.' The concierge ushered them both to the other side of the corridor, standing with them, as they each gestured to the other to go first in the line of two.

'Anyone else?' Apparently not. 'Okay, I'll be coming down the line with paper, so you can write your questions down. I'll be holding a meeting this afternoon and they'll all be addressed there.'

A couple of women opened their handbags, withdrawing paper and pens, handing spares out to the people next to them in the queue. Everyone was calm now and starting to look at the person next to them instead of just themselves, which was exactly what Rafe needed.

He ducked into the consulting room, apologising to Mel's patient for the intrusion, and fetched a pad, grabbing up a handful of pens from the holder on the desk. Then he started to work quickly down the line, giving out paper and asking again if anyone had any medical concerns that he needed to know about.

This was exactly why he needed to keep his distance from Mel. In a crowd of people where one little boy needed to see a doctor, and two others had medical queries, he'd been able to see only her. Allowing his own attraction for her to run riot and take over his thoughts would only get in the way of what he was here to do.

And feeling again what he'd felt when he'd first met Annu allowed the possibility of feeling what he'd felt when she'd died. It might not be entirely logical to put himself into the role of Mel's protector, but Rafe's instincts seemed to have come to a different decision. That alone was more terrifying than the most ferocious of storms.

'Okay?' Half an hour later Rafe returned to the consulting room, finding Mel sitting alone behind the desk.

'Yes, the boy had been sick a couple of times this morning. I think it's a stomach upset from unfamiliar food rather than a bug, but I've called

Mr Manike and asked him to arrange for the family to be isolated for the time being just in case. There's no fever and I'll check back later on how he's doing.'

Rafe nodded. That wasn't really what he'd wanted to know. He'd been hoping that Mel might tell him how *she* was. Clearly she preferred to keep that to herself.

'I've spoken to a couple of people who were concerned about their medication. No problems there, but it's good to know who we need to keep an eye on.'

Mel nodded. It seemed that she had a better idea of their current priorities than he did at the moment. 'A board would be useful, so we can have all that information in one place. I wonder if Mr Manike has something we could use?'

'I expect so, I'll go and ask him. I've already spoken to him briefly about holding a meeting this afternoon to address some of the questions that people have, and he thinks that's a good idea. He's going to send a couple of pairs of scrubs down for you as well.'

Mel looked at him steadily. No surprise, no questions. Her face was devoid of emotion, and Rafe suspected this was a strategy on her part. Something was going on behind the façade that she didn't want him to know about.

'The doctor who usually visits the island uses

them, and he has some that he ordered for her. Looking the part can help in these situations. It gives people confidence.'

She nodded. Mel hadn't had any reservations in telling him exactly what was going on in her head when they'd first met, and he felt shut out now.

'Gives me confidence too.'

That was as far as Rafe felt he could go in encouraging her to talk, but Mel didn't bite.

'You seem to be doing just fine.' She gestured towards the paper in his hand. 'If you give me the questions I'll organise them into a list, while you go and see if you can rustle up an information board and some marker pens.'

That was a polite invitation to leave. He should take it.

'Okay. I'll be with Mr Manike if you want me...' Rafe was sure she wouldn't, and he should take this opportunity of severing himself from the rapidly growing feelings that threatened to turn his world upside down.

CHAPTER FOUR

RAFE DAVENPORT.

Mel had accompanied her young patient and his mother back to their room, and made sure he was settled and comfortable. Then she'd returned, taking refuge behind the authority of the large desk in the consulting room. Since her own defences were so low at the moment she needed something to fend him off.

Concentrating on a whiteboard and scrubs, neither of which were strictly necessary at the moment, had done the trick and Rafe had left her alone. Mel considered the idea. She shouldn't need to fend Rafe off at all. He was a doctor and that meant they were working towards the same thing. She should be pleased that he was here, and that she didn't have to face what was coming on her own.

Maybe it was yet another lesson in what she could, and couldn't, deal with. She was afraid of the oncoming storm and what havoc that might wreak, but that was a normal and reasonable reaction to real threats and she could deal with that. A pregnant woman was a concern, but she was confident that she could meet Zeena's needs. The challenge brought only a heightened sense of concentration, not the thoughtless mess of panic that had threatened to render her helpless and useless when she'd found herself caught up in the crowd of shouting people.

Rafe Davenport…?

Mel swallowed hard as her hands began to shake suddenly. Rafe was the trigger, the thing she couldn't deal with. She closed her eyes, trying to breathe slowly through the panic.

It couldn't be a coincidence that the last time she'd felt so anxious was when she'd been with Michael. She'd had relationships since then, but she'd made sure that they were all polite and convenient, with unchallenging men who in truth weren't any more than just friends. But polite and convenient simply wasn't possible with a gorgeous adventurer like Rafe. Her emotions were getting the better of her and she had no idea where that might lead.

Rafe was the kind of man who could push a well-ordered life into chaos. His challenging unpredictability didn't just make her feel suddenly alive, it provoked the kind of anxiety reaction that could stop her dead in her tracks.

Enough. She had a handle on this now, and she needed to do something to work off the fight or flight feeling that was still pounding in her veins. Her anxiety stemmed from situations where she felt out of control, and Mel needed to do something, *anything,* to convince herself that she had some traction over her life.

The list of questions could wait. She wanted to be on her feet and doing something. The row of cupboards on the wall, some of which could only be reached with the help of a small stepladder stowed neatly in the corner, was much more inviting. It would be useful to know what was available, and where it was kept.

She started at one end, opening each door in turn and making a mental note of what was where. There was a cupboard full of dressings, that could be called into use for anything from a cut finger to a broken limb. An ordered mind had thought everything through, and provided all kinds of diagnostic and examination equipment. And…

It made sense. This was an island, and there was no possibility of popping around the corner to the nearest chemist. People were on holiday, so romance probably vied with stomach bugs as the most common ailment a doctor had to deal with. And it was nice to offer a bit of variety.

But was a full height cupboard's worth of condoms really necessary?

Mel didn't get the chance to investigate any further. A knock sounded on the door and she banged the cupboard door shut before calling to whoever was waiting outside. The manager, Mr Manike, entered, carrying a bundle wrapped in paper.

'Pink or blue, Dr Murphy?' He smiled, putting the package down on the desk and opening it.

'What...?' Mel's mind was still on the range of condoms. Mr Manike brought her back down to earth with a bump by withdrawing two pairs of scrubs, still in their plastic wrappers.

Pink had the kind of friendly feel about it that would be great for delivering a baby. Blue was a colour that indicated seniority in her own hospital, and that might apply a splash of confidence in her dealings with Rafe.

'May I take one of each, please, Mr Manike?'

'Of course.' Mr Manike deposited an extra pair of each colour onto the desk for good measure. 'I hope they will fit. I order a medium woman's size for our usual doctor.'

'That's fine, thank you.' Mostly scrubs came in whatever size you could manage to get into, but Mr Manike's quiet attention to detail was very calming.

'I have also taken the liberty of bringing one of our usual doctor's white jackets. I am sure she would offer it if she were here. Freshly laundered, with not too much starch.'

'Perfect.' Mel grinned at the thought that the amount of starch was going to matter when caught in the terrifying centre of a storm. 'Not too much starch is just right, thank you. Do you know where Dr Davenport is, by any chance?'

'I spoke to him briefly on my way here about a whiteboard and pens, and I believe he is now with one of our work teams discussing how best to secure the sea plane. He tells me that you are dealing with a list of questions in preparation for the proposed meeting this afternoon.' Mr Manike withdrew a sheet of paper from his pocket. 'Here is the user name and password for the laptop our regular doctor uses, in case you need it.'

Mel hadn't even thought of the laptop that she'd pushed to one side on the desk. 'Thank you, that's useful.'

'We are asking all of the guests in the water cabins to pack their things, and are arranging for suitable accommodation in the main building. I have arranged for a room to be put at your disposal.'

Breath of fresh air. Fresh air that Mel could actually make some use of without her chest beginning to heave with the beginnings of panic.

Mr Manike's painstaking efficiency was a fine antidote to Rafe.

'Thank you again. I may stay here in the medical suite, so I'm available for anyone who needs me. Is there a camp bed that I could use?'

'The medical suite does have accommodation for visiting doctors, but you are a guest, Dr Murphy.'

'Right now I'm a doctor, and I'd like to be here.'

Mr Manike nodded, suddenly brisk now that he'd said all he'd come to say. 'As you wish. Please let me know if there is anything I can do to make you more comfortable.'

As the door closed quietly behind him, Mel sucked in a breath. She could decide not to dwell on the light in Rafe's eyes, the way he made her feel so alive when he smiled. Nor did she need to take any notice of his body, or his scent, and definitely not how the touch of his fingers might feel. She could deal with the situation she'd found herself in, and she could deal with Rafe as well.

'Three o'clock.'

Mel had turned her attention to the list of questions and then gone to collect her things from her water cabin. As she wheeled her suitcase back to the hotel, she made a point of ignoring the fact that Rafe was helping board up the windows of the medical suite. She wasn't having any truck with *distractingly gorgeous* and Rafe was one of those men who seemed at his best whenever physical exertion was involved.

'What's happening at three?' She shaded her eyes as she looked up at him.

'The meeting.' Rafe swung down the ladder, wiping his forearm across his brow as he walked over to where she stood. *Very* annoyingly sexy, but he didn't seem to be able to help it.

'Ah. I've typed the list of questions if you want to look over it beforehand.'

Rafe shook his head. 'Thanks. I'll wing it and work down the list when I get there.'

She should have expected that. 'Line everyone up in a queue if they start to get rowdy...?'

That sounded less like a joke than she'd meant it to be, and more like a criticism. That really wasn't fair. Rafe had dealt with the situation a lot better than she had. The look of silent amusement on his face told her that he knew it as well, but he had the decency not to say so.

'You did what needed to be done. I guess instinct takes over in these kinds of situations, and everyone tends to act out of character.' It was as close as Mel was going to get to an apology, because apologies required explanation. Rafe had obviously noticed her own loss of control but perhaps he wouldn't mention it.

He shrugged, changing the subject. 'Has Mr Manike sorted you out with a room for the night?'

'I'd like to stay close to Zeena. There's accommodation for doctors in the medical suite, isn't there?'

'There is.'

Rafe turned, signalling to the men he was working with that he would be a minute, and then opening the door that led into the building. He led her through the consulting room and down the corridor, past the patient rooms, to a door at the end.

There were three comfortable-looking beds, each with curtains that could be drawn around them for privacy. On one side an open door led to a small kitchen, and Rafe gestured towards another closed door on the other side of the room.

'There's a shower room through there, although it's important not to use taps or showers during an electrical storm, so the staff will be around later on to put tape across the basin and shower cubicle in the bathroom.'

'Is that going to be enough in the guest rooms?'

'No, there's always someone who decides that

a shower is worth risking a jolt if lightning hits the water system, so they're locking and taping bathroom doors in the guest rooms. But here we'll need to be able to wash in case of any medical emergencies, so they'll be delivering a couple of plastic barrels of water and a bowl, that we can use. Is your phone charged?'

'Um…yes, I think so. Can we use our phones?'

'Yeah, if the phone mast stays in one piece. I've got some batteries and a portable charger, but we need to go easy on any phone use because we don't know how long this is going to last. The staff are covering and taping electrical sockets as well.'

'Right. No running water, no electrical devices. What about light?'

'There's emergency lighting here and in most areas of the hotel, and that's powered by the main generator, so we should be okay there.' Rafe stepped forward, picking up a small holdall that lay beside one of the beds. 'I'll let you settle in…'

'Wait. Where are you going to sleep?' Rafe had clearly staked his claim to one of the beds, in the expectation that Mel would be occupying one of the guest rooms.

A flash of embarrassment showed in his eyes. 'I'll…um…find somewhere.'

This was ridiculous. And an opportunity to

show herself, or maybe Rafe, she wasn't sure which, that she could spend the night a few feet away from him without dissolving into sleepless panic.

'That's not necessary. I went to medical school, the same as you did.'

He chuckled. 'So tired that you could sleep anywhere?'

'And with anyone.' Mel bit her lip. That hadn't come out quite the way she'd meant it to, but at least Rafe's expression didn't give any indication that he'd registered the faux pas.

'If you're sure.'

'Positive.' Mel walked over to the bed that was furthest from the one his holdall had been next to and parked her case next to it. 'This will be fine, and it's probably just as well if we're in the same place if we're needed.'

He nodded and put his own bag back down again. 'Right then. I'll finish up with the windows and then I should probably clean up a bit before the meeting.'

It wouldn't do to have Rafe looking this good in front of a whole hotel full of guests. They might miss any number of important pieces of safety and medical information.

'I'll leave you to it then, and check in on Zeena again, to see how she's doing.'

Rafe nodded. It seemed they *could* work out

a basic split in responsibilities if they put their minds to it, and that was all good. Smiling at him didn't seem so very challenging now, and Mel even allowed her eyes to linger on his back for a few extra moments as he walked away.

Mel had spent an hour with Zeena and her husband. Speaking to the couple together gave her the opportunity to ask a few more questions about their expectations for the birth, and to make sure that she'd missed nothing in terms of providing a nurturing environment for them that took account of both their personal wishes and their Muslim faith.

Then Haroon looked at his watch. 'Time to go. Would you like to come, Zeena?'

Zeena shifted uncomfortably. 'Yes, I'd like to take a walk.'

Instead of walking up and down the corridor for a while, it seemed that Haroon and Zeena had a particular destination in mind. Mel followed them to the restaurant, where they joined the rest of the islanders in one corner, for Rafe's health and safety talk.

'Surely you know everything he's going to say already?' Mel leaned across, murmuring to Zeena.

'Yes. But we have come to support him.' Zeena smiled. 'Dr Davenport will tell everyone that everything will be all right, and we will agree.'

That sounded like a plan. And when Rafe joined Mr Manike, who was waiting to start the meeting, the room fell silent. He looked the part. A clean, crisp shirt and a pair of chinos. Hair still slightly wet from the shower, which tamed his curls a little. A broad, reassuring smile and... Rafe just had a presence. It was difficult not to feel that he knew exactly what he was doing, and that next to him was the safest place you could possibly be.

He ran through everything, taking in all of the questions that had been asked and giving clear and concise instructions about what to do in response to a number of different scenarios. Watching out for any wildlife that might seek shelter in the hotel building. Staying inside, even after the storm seemed to be passing, and waiting until the hotel team had pronounced it was safe to leave the building. Calling for help immediately if they were ill or injured in any way, and waiting for the medical team to come to them. He made it all seem easy.

'In short...' he gave a smile that would bolster anyone's spirits '...sit tight, do as the hotel staff ask you, and you'll be able to resume your holidays as soon as the storm subsides. And you'll have a story to take back home with you.'

A ripple of laughter ran around the restaurant. Rafe invited further questions but everyone seemed content with what they'd heard. Zeena was nodding, her hand protectively across her stomach, and Mel had to admit that if she was smiling then there couldn't be a great deal to worry about.

'Oh, and by the way. We're fortunate that Dr Mel Murphy is here on holiday, and we'll both be on call tonight, although we're confident we won't be seeing any of you in our official capacity. But if you need her, Mel's here too.'

It was probably a good idea to point her out, so that people knew who she was. The clapping that rippled around the restaurant in response to Rafe's gesture of applause wasn't strictly necessary though, and Mel shifted uncomfortably in her seat. But Zeena patted her on the back, beaming, and the islanders' smiles seemed to be setting the tone for the behaviour of the hotel guests.

'When *is* the storm expected to be over?' Mel asked as they strolled back to the medical suite together, and Rafe shrugged.

'I said I can't give an exact time. Mother Nature goes at her own pace.'

'Now that it's moving closer, I imagine that it would be easier to predict, though.'

Rafe opened the door of the consulting room

for her, waiting until Mel had walked inside and he'd closed the door behind them. 'There is some indication. The Meteorological Office says that there's a front moving in the other direction, and when it meets the storm it may stop it in its tracks.'

Cold fingers closed around her heart. 'Where will that be?'

'It's impossible to say right now. Maybe here, maybe thirty or forty miles east of the island. But if it's here, then the storm will last longer than just one night. Maybe two to three days. We'll have to wait and see. I've spoken with Mr Manike and we don't see any point in alarming people until we actually know the situation.'

Mel nodded. Everyone was calm at the moment and an atmosphere of camaraderie seemed to be developing. Maybe it *was* better to say nothing until they were sure. 'Okay. Thanks for telling me. Do the islanders know?'

'The islanders know that you can never really predict exactly how a storm's going to behave, or how long it'll last. They'll tell you to wait and see, and that it'll be over when it's over.'

'And that everything's going to be okay?' Suddenly Mel really needed to hear him say that. If Rafe said it, then perhaps she'd believe him.

'You're a doctor, you know it's never a good

idea to make blanket predictions.' He fell silent, looking at her thoughtfully. Maybe he saw the terror that Mel was trying so hard to hide. 'But yeah. Everything's going to be okay.'

Mel was an enigma. She seemed so certain of herself, so capable, and yet Rafe couldn't forget that sudden glimpse of her vulnerable side. He'd been unable to shake the feeling that there was something wrong, something beyond the fact that no one with any sense was completely unafraid in the face of an emergency of a kind they'd never experienced before.

When a short queue of people had formed outside the consulting room door, mostly wanting reassurance, he'd wondered if he should deal with them, but she'd arranged for a line of chairs to be put out and chased him away. Activity seemed to quell her fears, and Rafe needed to get the sea plane under cover before the storm hit.

He changed out of his clean shirt, dragging a T-shirt over his head, and then rounded up the men he'd been working with to fix the storm shutters. It took a couple of hours to unload the medical supplies and move the light aircraft out of the water and up the beach, to a large out-building that was used to store the hotel's water sports equipment. Space had been found to accommodate the plane, and he secured it alongside the boats and kayaks that were being tied down to minimise any damage.

The wind was beginning to pick up now, kicking up small plumes of fine white sand on the beach. The sky was dark with clouds, coming in from the east, and Rafe made his way back to the hotel, ordering a crate of soft drinks from the bar for the men who'd been working all day, to wash some of the dust from their throats. Everything was ready, they'd done as much as they could, and now they just had to wait.

When he popped in to Zeena's room he half expected to find Mel there, but she wasn't. Zeena assured him that she was quite all right and that the baby would come whenever it came, telling him that Mel had been here but that she'd gone to see if she could get a couple of hours' sleep before the storm hit.

Something made him turn and walk to the end of the corridor. Maybe the thought that even the steeliest of hearts found it difficult to sleep before a storm, however sensible the suggestion seemed. Maybe some instinct telling him that he needed to know where Mel was and that she was all right.

The door was slightly ajar and the doctors'

ready room seemed dark and quiet. Maybe Mel really was sleeping. Rafe hesitated in the doorway and then he caught the sound of a ragged breath.

She was crying. Alone in the dark, where no one could see her.

CHAPTER FIVE

THE QUIET BEFORE the storm. Mel had supposed that it was just a figure of speech, but it really *was* quiet. The air was heavy and humid, seeming to press down on her like a smothering blanket.

She'd eaten dinner with Zeena and her husband and, after checking her blood pressure and reassuring her that she was in great shape, left the couple alone together for the evening. Even if she didn't sleep, Mel reckoned that a couple of hours' rest might stand her in good stead for whatever was to come that night, but had found that it was too hot to slip under a blanket, and not comforting enough to lie on the bed without something to cover her.

The dark silence was corrosive, eating into her shell of measured confidence. She lay on her left side, then her right, and then on her back, and when she'd run out of positions that might potentially be comfortable Mel went to fetch a bottle of water from the kitchen, finding that even though the refrigerator was unplugged the bottles inside were still cool. As she closed the door a low rumble of distant thunder sounded. A mile away? Two? Twenty? The uncertainty of all this was killing her.

Backing out of the kitchen, she stumbled back towards her bed, pulling the curtains around it. Maybe she should call Amy...

Mel had decided not to call her daughter, on the basis that the storm would be over before Amy could possibly worry about not being able to contact her for their promised weekly catchup. But if the storm lasted for days then communications might be affected for goodness only knew how long. Amy might call and then decide to look at the weather reports for this region.

She could call Amy and tell her that she was having a wonderful time, but that reception on her phone wasn't great and so not to worry if she didn't hear from her. Mel took her phone from her bag, calling Amy's number. Nothing. The phone was charged and even though she had only one reception bar that should be enough. She dialled again. Then again. She so badly wanted to hear Amy's voice.

She had to pull herself together. If she was crying when she called then Amy would know that something was up, and she'd worry. Mel took a couple of deep breaths and then tried again. The call didn't connect yet again, and Mel sank down onto the floor, the wall at her back giving her at least some measure of security.

She didn't know how long she'd stayed there for, her knees pulled up in front of her and her head in her hands, trying to stop herself from crying. When a soft footstep and the instinct that someone else was in the room made her open her eyes she was blinded for a moment by light streaming in from the doorway.

Why hadn't she thought to draw the privacy curtains around her bed? As her eyes adjusted to the light, she saw Rafe's solid shadow and froze, panic driving every excuse that she could think of for sitting on the floor in the darkness from her head.

Maybe he'd come to fetch something and he wouldn't notice her. Mel held her breath.

'I could do with someone to talk to. The waiting's getting to me.'

His voice was soft, almost tender. No…it was definitely tender. And even if this was very clearly his way of making her feel better, she didn't care because even his silhouette was reassuring. Mel took a sip of water from the bottle beside her to clear her throat.

'There's a spare seat here. Help yourself.'

'Thanks. I appreciate it.' He sat down on the floor next to her.

The foreboding shadows *were* suddenly less intimidating. And half-light might make her tears a little less obvious. Although Rafe was clearly aware of them, since he'd handed her a clean tissue. Mel wiped her eyes and blew her nose.

'Thanks. Did you get your sea plane sorted?'

'Yep. She's tied down in one of the outhouses, with the boats.' He nodded towards the phone, still clutched in her hand. 'Been trying to call someone?'

'My daughter. Amy.'

He leaned over, taking the phone from her grasp and putting it down on the floor between them. 'And what were you thinking of saying to her?'

Mel shrugged. 'Probably best to tell her all about it when I get home. I couldn't get through, anyway.'

'Yeah, everyone's either on the internet or trying to phone home at the moment, and getting stressed out about it. Why don't you message her? Your phone will connect as soon as there's a signal and you don't have to keep dialling.'

'Yeah. Later maybe, when I've worked out what to say.'

'That's a good idea too. Zeena's okay?'

Mel doubted that he didn't already know how Zeena was. He was probably just trying to take her mind off everything else for a moment, but the ploy seemed to be working.

'Yes, her vitals are stable, and the baby will be along any time now. I thought that she and her husband could do with some quiet time together.' Mel pressed her lips together, feeling the embarrassment of the situation seep into her. 'I'm not usually this edgy about waiting for things to happen.'

'No? I am, every time. It's the downside of being ready, I reckon. I wouldn't have it any other way, but my instinct tells me I'd rather be doing something.'

'Me too. Nothing's ever as bad as you think it's going to be in your head.'

Rafe nodded. He was so solid, and he exuded safety. Mel could feel her heart begin to steady, just at the sound of his voice, and his scent. A trace of machine oil and hard work, mingling with the stronger smell of soap. She would allow herself this, if it meant that she could meet the night ahead.

'So how's London these days? It's been a while since I was there.'

'It's much the same as it ever was, I guess. Always changing.'

Rafe smiled. 'Yeah. That was what I liked

about it. Always the same, and yet always something new.'

'How long since you've been there?' There was a trace of reminiscence in his voice that said it had probably been a while.

'Eight…no, ten years. I took my son when he was fifteen, just to show him where his dad came from.'

'You have a son?'

Rafe shifted, taking his phone from his back pocket. Flipping through photographs, he found the one he was looking for and passed the phone over to Mel. A golden-skinned, dark-haired young man, who clearly shared his father's temperament. He was standing on the floats of a sea plane, much like the one that Rafe had arrived in, grinning at the camera, a deep blue cloudless sky in the background.

'Ash has just qualified as a doctor. He's working in Colombo at the moment.'

'He's like you.'

Rafe leaned over to look at the phone, his shoulder touching hers. 'You think so? I always reckoned he'd got the best of the bargain and took after my wife.'

His wife. Mel wondered whether she should feel that there was one lucky lady, or someone with a challenge on her hands. Whatever the case, Mel really shouldn't be feeling any of the

warmth that his mere presence seemed to en-
gender. She excused herself by remembering
she'd been doing her best not to feel anything
for Rafe ever since she'd met him.

'He looks as if he's just finished doing one
thing and about to do another.'

That made him laugh. 'Yeah. If I remember
rightly, he had just completed a few repairs and
was about to take the plane up when I took that
photograph.'

'Your wife's Sri Lankan?'

'Yes, she was. Annu died when Ash was ten
months old. Cancer.'

And he still felt it. Of course he did. Time
healed but it never dismissed that kind of pain
entirely. There was a matter-of-factness about
the way that Rafe said it, but it couldn't hide the
quiver in his voice.

'I'm so sorry. That must have been terrible
for you.'

'Yeah. The first few years were the worst, but
having Ash to look after did a lot in encouraging me to pull myself together.'

'You've brought him up alone?'

Rafe's lips quirked in a slight smile. 'I suppose if by *alone* you mean with the help of Annu's extended family, some of whom weren't
strictly speaking related to her, then yeah. I
brought him up alone. They're the reason I

stayed in Sri Lanka. I don't have much family back in England and Ash needed them as much as he did me.'

'No plans to go back now, though?' Rafe seemed so at home here.

'No. You can get to love Sri Lanka very easily. And there's enough to keep me occupied.'

'Flying around, dropping in on people who might need you?' He shrugged, and Mel let the question drop, reaching for her own phone. 'I've pictures of my own.'

'Oh. Let me see…'

Mel flipped to the picture of Amy that she particularly liked, taken in the porch at the church, smiling up at her new husband. 'That's my daughter, Amy.'

Rafe took the phone, a broad grin spreading across his face. 'I can tell. She's a lot like you. Beautiful.'

A little sizzle of heat chased the last of the chills of the night away. People often commented on how much Amy and Mel were alike, and if Rafe thought Amy beautiful…

She dismissed the thought. What else was anyone supposed to say when presented with a photograph of a bride?

'You must have been very young when you had her.'

That could be taken as a compliment as well,

if you really tried. Mel decided not to try. 'I had Amy after I'd completed first year at university. I was able to defer my studies for a year, but my relationship with Amy's father broke up. My family came to the rescue too. They took us in and looked after Amy so that I could go back to university.'

'It makes all the difference in the world, doesn't it.' Rafe was scrolling through the photographs on his phone and when he found the one he wanted he handed it to Mel. 'That's Ash at five years old, with his grandparents.'

'He looks as if he's having a lot of fun with that paddling pool. Can I swipe?'

He chuckled. 'As much as you like. Ash always gives me a hard time over loading all of the photos of him when he was little, each time I get a new phone.'

'They don't understand, do they? When Amy starts her own family, she'll get it.' Mel found the folder that contained all of Amy's childhood photographs and handed her phone to Rafe.

'She's very cute. Can *I* swipe?'

'Knock yourself out. We'll see who gets to the end first…'

Something was growing, here in the darkness. Something tender, that was reflected in the faces in the photographs. She and Rafe had found common ground, and it was in the thing that meant the most to them both. Sitting close, feeling the brush of his arm against hers, seemed natural and reassuring.

His phone rang and Mel jumped. He leaned across, taking it from her hand, and she felt his scent wash through her senses, like an intoxicating wave. Maybe it was just as well that these moments were coming to an end. He listened for a moment, and then nodded.

'Okay. We'll be straight there.' He ended the call, turning to Mel. 'Looks as if we're done waiting.'

He was suddenly all movement, and there was no time to ask why his phone should be working when hers wasn't. At least the intermittent nature of the connection had saved Mel from doing anything that she'd regret later. Rafe got to his feet and when he held out his hand to her she took it, her legs and back a little stiff from sitting so long, hunched on the floor.

As he led the way swiftly out of the doctors' ready room the sound of thunder crashed around them, almost above their heads.

CHAPTER SIX

As he passed Zeena's door, Rafe knocked and briefly looked in on her. She and her husband were sitting together playing draughts and clearly the baby wasn't going to be coming in the next fifteen minutes. Hopefully by then the current number one on his to-do list would be resolved.

And hopefully the impulse that time spent with Mel was the most important thing in the world would have sunk back into perspective as well. There had been a closeness between them that he hadn't allowed himself to feel in twenty-five years, and which he'd had no intention of allowing himself to feel again. His marriage had been a good one, a once in a lifetime experience. If he ever wavered in that belief, he only had to remember the pain that Annu's death had caused.

He led the way to Mr Manike's office, knocking on the door and opening it before he heard the call to come inside. Mr Manike was sitting in the small anteroom, in front of a whole bank of screens which showed the feeds from the various CCTV cameras.

'What's happening?' Mel stepped forward, addressing her question to Mr Manike, and Rafe couldn't help but smile. The side of her that took life by the scruff of the neck and hung on tight was back.

'Look. Here.' Mr Manike indicated one of the screens, which showed a view of the lagoon and the water cabins. Mel leant forward to study the exact area that he was pointing to, and Rafe looked over her shoulder. He was crowding her a little so that he could see properly, but she didn't move away. He fancied she even moved a little closer.

'What's that? A light, in one of the cabins?' Mel asked.

'Looks like it.' Rafe stared at the glimmering point of white light on the black and white image. 'Someone's left a light on in one of the water cabins?'

'Maybe… Keep looking.' Mr Manike was still staring at the screen.

Then they saw it. A brief shadow passed in front of the light and Mel gasped, putting her hand to her mouth. 'There's someone out there!'

Someone who was clearly not very mindful of their own safety. 'Who's staying in that cabin?'

Mr Manike pulled a sheet of paper towards him. 'Mr and Mrs Cartwright. Young honeymooners. Mr Cartwright has been very keen in his participation in our more extreme water sports.'

Young honeymooners out for kicks. Rafe could imagine the kind of tragedy that might lead to all too well.

'Okay. I'll go and get them.' He turned, walking out into the main office, where a bundle of sou'westers was hanging on the peg that was usually reserved for Mr Manike's jacket. Rafe selected the largest and pulled it on.

'Wait... Rafe!' Mel caught his arm and instinctively he shook himself free. This was something he needed to do alone.

'Stay here. Zeena needs you...' She understood the unspoken as well as he did. If anything happened to him, then there would still be a doctor here to look after Zeena. He was largely surplus to requirements, the man who had lived when his talented wife, who had so much more to give to the world than he did, had died.

And he wouldn't let Mel risk herself. He was beginning to need that, more than he could admit to. Rafe heard her call his name, exasperation sounding in her voice, and he ignored her. Mel could be as exasperated as she liked, but he needed to have her safe.

He strode out of Mr Manike's office to the private door that led out onto the beach, nodding at the two men who were keeping an eye on it to make sure that no one used the only way out of here that wasn't boarded shut. As he pushed out into the oncoming storm, the wind pushed back. But he was stronger.

He *had* to be stronger, because there were two young people out there who might just be making the biggest mistake of their lives.

Typical! *Typical!* Just when Mel was thinking that Rafe was someone that she could trust, he snapped that connection like a dry twig under his foot. It was all the more hurtful because Michael had done that again and again, until finally Mel had questioned her every thought and deed.

'Can't you stop him?' She turned on Mr Manike in frustration.

'I think that any man might do the same.' Mr Manike was staring at the CCTV images, tracking Rafe's movements from one camera to another.

Not quite any man. She suspected that Rafe was a little more disposed to stepping in and playing the part of a lone hero than most, and it was irritating when they both had a job to do. The years had taught Mel to distinguish between her own shortcomings and those of others, and this one she could lay squarely at Rafe's feet.

And what Rafe didn't seem to grasp was that if there was no stopping him, then there was no stopping Mel either. 'Have you got two volunteers, to go outside with me? Strong…'

Mr Manike considered the matter and then nodded. 'Of course.'

Clearly this had been his original plan, because in response to his call two burly men appeared, clad in waterproofs. Mel grabbed one of the sou'westers from the peg and slipped it on, finding that it wasn't so big that she couldn't find her hands somewhere in the sleeves.

'Right then.' She turned to the volunteers, one of whom she recognised from behind the bar last night. 'You're happy to go out there with me? I may need your help.'

'Don't worry, miss.' Adil, the bartender, smiled at her. 'Mushan and I will get you out there and back inside again, no problem.'

'Thank you. I want you to be careful and not to take any unnecessary risks. We can't help anyone else if we're not in one piece ourselves.' Mel wasn't quite sure how that applied to help-

ing Rafe, because right now she was so furious
with him she could march out there alone and
pluck him from the eye of the storm. But Adil
and Mushan weren't to be involved in that part
of the operation.

Mr Manike produced a pair of safety glasses
and Mel put them on, tucking the holding strap
around the back of her head. It seemed she was
about the only person who didn't quite know
what to expect from the conditions outside, because Adil and Mushan both withdrew similar
protection from their pockets.

As soon as she stepped through the door and
onto the beach the wind almost knocked her
off her feet, and Adil reached out to steady her.
There was sand too, stinging her skin as it was
whipped up by the wind, and Mel pulled the
high collar of her sou'wester across her mouth.
Together the three figures made their way
down the beach and onto the wooden walkway
that led to the water cabins. It creaked alarm-
ingly under their weight and water was slop-
ping against their feet, but the structure seemed
sound enough and Adil nodded, clearly deem-
ing it safe.

They were making better progress than Rafe,
able to support each other as the wind buffeted
them. Mel kept her eyes on him, catching her
breath as he staggered in response to a partic-

ularly strong gust of wind. But he regained his footing and as he did so he looked behind him.

His gesture was crystal-clear in its meaning. Go back. Adil and Mushan hesitated, but when Mel pressed on ahead they followed her. When they reached Rafe he leaned towards her, shouting to make himself heard.

'Thought I told you not to come out here...'

'I thought *I* told you not to go alone...' Mel yelled back at him, wondering if this was going to turn into an argument.

But Rafe shrugged suddenly, taking her arm and guiding her along the walkway. Mel had to admit that it was very welcome, as the waves that were sloshing against her ankles were getting stronger now, threatening to whip her feet out from under her.

They could see the light in the furthest cabin more clearly now, and it seemed to be coming from the back of the structure, where the bedroom was situated. Maybe the young bride and groom had left something behind and decided to return for it. She couldn't imagine what could be so important that they would risk their safety for it, but people did thoughtless things at times.

Rafe reached the sliding doors of the cabin, feeling inside his jacket for a pocket multi-tool, and made short work of the lock. He opened the door, bundling Mel inside, and then followed

Adil and Mushan, sliding the door closed behind them. The sudden absence of wind and noise almost took her breath away, and it was a moment before she could compose herself enough to look around.

'Mate… Trust me, sex in a storm sounds a great deal better than it actually is. Do us all a favour and get your wife out of here.' Rafe's voice was suddenly relaxed, almost jocular.

Mel looked up and saw the object of his comments standing by the sliding doors that led to the bedroom. A young man, with sun-blond hair and an impressive tan, wearing only a cocky smile. When he realised that Mel was regarding him, his grin became broader and he slowly covered his manhood with his hand.

'I wouldn't bother. Dr Murphy's undoubtedly seen anything you have to offer. Put your clothes on and let's be going.'

It seemed that Rafe's tone was working, and the young man started to turn. But then a young, equally blonde woman appeared in the bedroom doorway, clad only in a very skimpy towel. She yelped at the sight of the three burly men and ducked behind her husband. Adil and Mushan immediately turned their gazes to the floor, and even Rafe seemed to be making some effort to look somewhere else while still keeping control of the situation.

'Oh, please...'

Mel hadn't come out here to play games with the couple, and neither had the men, despite their obvious attempts at gentlemanly behaviour. She stepped forward, taking the woman by the shoulders and propelling her into the bedroom. A pair of woman's jeans lay tangled on the floor with a sweater, and Mel picked them up.

'Get these on. Now.'

'Hey. Don't sweat it...' The man had followed and was thankfully stepping into his own jeans.

'Enough with the attitude!' Rafe's brisk words floated through the open doorway, unmistakably an order now. 'Do as the lady says.'

'I think we should go, Ty...' The woman had pulled her sweater over her head and was wriggling into her jeans. 'This cabin isn't quite as stable as we thought...'

Just how stable had they thought a wooden cabin would be, suspended over the water in a gale? Mel never got the chance to ask, because a loud crash sounded against the floor-to-ceiling window, showering the bed with broken glass. Rafe was there suddenly, his arm around Mel's shoulders as he shepherded everyone out of the bedroom.

Mr and Mrs Cartwright suddenly got the message, in the most graphic way possible. Ty pulled on his sweater and Rafe ducked back into the bedroom, fetching the two pairs of trainers that were lying on the floor. Mel inspected both pairs for any broken glass before handing them to Ty and his wife to hurriedly put on.

'We stay together, right?' Rafe had obviously decided that the couple needed no more cajoling and was taking off his own sou'wester and wrapping it around the young woman's shoulders. 'You do exactly as Adil and Mushan tell you. Without question.'

'Yes, okay.' Ty was clearly doing his best not to lose too much face. 'Do as they say, Em.'

Mel rolled her eyes. For a moment Rafe's gaze caught hers, and his mouth twitched in a crooked smile. Then he opened the door of the cabin. Adil and Mushan went first and then Rafe beckoned to Ty and Em to follow them. When it was Mel's turn she felt Rafe's reassuring hand on her arm.

They were halfway along the walkway, back to the safety of the beach, when suddenly the wind seemed to drop a little. A moment of silence, and then the rain started, so heavy that it felt as if someone had just tipped a bucket of water over Mel's head. Ty let go of his wife, raising his arm to shield his face against the onslaught. Em staggered a little and lost her footing, falling onto the walkway. Before Rafe could reach her, a wave sloshed across the boards and she slid into the sea.

In normal circumstances that wasn't going to hurt anyone. Last evening, Mel had seen people stepping off the walkways and wading in the warm sea to their cabins. But now the waves were higher and could very easily knock someone off their feet, and who knew what kind of sharp objects were in the turbulent water?

But Rafe was there. She felt Adil take hold of her arm as Rafe swung his legs over the handrails and let himself down into the sea, where Em was struggling helplessly. When he grabbed her, lifting her out of the water, Mel saw blood mixed with the water that was running down his arms, but it was impossible to say whether it was his or Em's.

Mushan lifted Em over the handrail, setting her back down on her feet. Mel ran her hands over the sou'wester, looking for any tears that might signify a wound.

'Are you all right? Can you keep walking?'

'Yes… I'm okay, I can walk.' Em nodded.

'Right then. We'll take a look at you as soon as we get inside.' Mel was watching as Rafe climbed back over the railings, breathing her own sigh of relief when he was safely back on the walkway. Together the small party made their way back to the beach and as they approached the door into the hotel it opened, willing hands pulling them inside.

Mel seemed in her element. She'd despatched him to the doctors' ready room, to wash off the grime, and had taken Em into one of the patient rooms, presumably for the same treatment. He drew a bowl full of water from the barrel that stood next to the hand basin and walked through to the shower room at the far end, putting the bowl on the tiled floor outside the cubicle. Rafe soaped his shoulders and arms, then picked up his flannel to wipe them, trying to avoid the areas that were already stinging from contact with soap and water.

The scrape on his forearm wasn't too bad but Rafe was pretty sure that the other wound would need stitches. Which was a shame because it was above his elbow on the back of his arm, which meant he couldn't reach it himself and he was going to have to ask Mel to stitch it for him. And the look she'd given him when she'd ordered him to go and clean himself up had left him in no doubt that she was still unhappy about his having gone out to fetch Ty and Em Cartwright on his own.

Hindsight was always twenty-twenty. He

probably could have managed alone, and he stood by the guiding principle of his actions. If one of them was going to take their chances out there, then it was going to be him.

He heard a knock at the outer door and it opened a crack. 'Hey. How are you doing in there?' Mel was standing outside the bathroom, calling in.

'Fine, thanks.'

'You're not absolutely fine, are you? You're bleeding.'

'And how would you know that?'

He heard a loud, rather theatrical sigh. 'Because I saw blood when you lifted Em out of the water. And I've just given her a thorough once-over and she doesn't have a mark on her.'

'Did she swallow any water?' Maybe he could keep the subject on Em's possible injuries until he was at least dry and felt a bit more able to face the world.

'She says not, but I'll keep an eye on her. And meanwhile…'

The bathroom door swung open. Rafe reached for the door to the shower room and banged it shut, hearing her footsteps outside.

'Hey…!'

'I thought it was nothing I hadn't seen before.' There was a trace of amusement in her voice.

Rafe rubbed his hand across his face, trying to wipe away his own smile.

'I don't want to bore you,' he called back to her.

'I'm sure you're underestimating yourself.' Mel was clearly intent on making the most of the fact that she was standing in between him and his clothes, which were in his bag at his bedside.

'It's generous of you to say so. I'll see you in the consulting room in ten minutes. If you wouldn't mind, I think I need a couple of stitches.'

'My pleasure. If you start feeling dizzy, call me.'

He was feeling dizzy already. Light-headed, and weak-kneed. None of that was anything to do with blood loss. It was more to do with the fact that Mel was just a few paces away from him.

'I'm sure you have something better to do than harangue me, Dr Murphy.'

'I'm sure I do, Dr Davenport.' He heard Mel's footsteps again, and the door closed behind her.

Rafe finished washing himself and walked through to inspect the wound on his arm in the mirror above the hand basin. It was still bleeding and he reached for a couple of paper hand-towels to press against it, before wrapping a towel awkwardly around his hips with one hand.

The towel probably wasn't strictly necessary. If Mel was going to torment him any more then he couldn't imagine that she'd lie in wait for him outside. Meeting him head-on seemed far more her style.

He smiled to himself grimly. Much as he liked crossing swords with Mel, this was one thing he wasn't going to compromise on.

She was very thorough, and very gentle. Rafe sat on the examination couch, rather more embarrassed than usual over the fact that Mel had stripped his T-shirt off to examine his shoulders and torso for any other signs of injury. She was currently sitting behind him, carefully pulling splinters of wood from the cut on his upper arm with the aid of a magnifying glass and a pair of tweezers.

'I think that's everything. You want to see for yourself?'

'I trust you.' Rafe was staring at the wall, wondering when Mel would decide that she'd been more than kind and he now deserved a telling-off.

'Really? You've picked *this* moment to trust me?' She murmured the words quietly, which made them seem all the more cutting, and Rafe sighed.

'Okay. You're angry, aren't you?'

'Yes, I'm angry. Hold still while I irrigate the wound and stitch it.'

In anyone else, the thought of angry stitches might have made him pause. But it seemed that Rafe *did* trust Mel enough to back off if emotion got the better of her. She'd already numbed the skin around his wound with a local anaesthetic and he felt only the cold dribble of antiseptic as it ran down towards his elbow, quickly mopped by a piece of cotton wool.

A slight push against his skin as the stitches went in. 'Five?' Rafe bit his tongue. Maybe he shouldn't question her judgement right now, or he was liable to find his lips stitched together.

'Six. If you decide to try any other stunts like the one you pulled tonight, I don't want you pulling them apart.'

'It wasn't a stunt, Mel. Someone needed to go out there, and it didn't make sense for the only two doctors in the place to go.'

'Hmm. Maybe we should both stay in separate rooms at all times, just in case something comes crashing through the ceiling.' The sixth stitch went in as smoothly as the other five and Mel reached round, handing him a mirror.

'That's great, thank you.' Rafe squinted at the six neat stitches. 'And you're taking it to ridiculous lengths. We need to work together and nothing's going to be crashing through the ceiling tonight. I just don't see that it's all that useful to deliberately put both of us at risk. I know my own capabilities.'

He pressed his lips together. Rafe hadn't wanted to bring up the moment when the clamour of a crowd of people around her had left Mel suddenly paralysed, because she clearly didn't want to talk about it. But it had happened and he couldn't ignore it.

'I get that. But you can't just decide you have a monopoly on mindless daring.' He felt the gentle sweep of her fingers as she dressed the wound and when Mel had finished Rafe went to pull his T-shirt back on.

'Wait...' He felt her hand on his shoulder. 'I'll dress that other scrape. It doesn't look as if it's going to stop bleeding unless it's covered.'

Now he could see her, carefully irrigating the deep graze on his forearm and securing a dressing over it. Somehow, she managed to be just as immaculate as she'd been before going out into a force eight gale and her hair still smelled faintly of roses.

'It's not mindless daring. What do you take me for?'

Her gaze flipped up towards his, giving him the inexplicable feeling that he was completely naked.

'I'm not sure what I take you for yet. What I

do know is that we're supposed to be working together and you didn't see any need to discuss our next move with me.'

'You mean we could have talked about it, and *then* decided that I'd go and you'd stay here. By which time that window could have shattered all over Ty and Em and we'd be doing more than just dressing a couple of scrapes on my arm.'

'No. Discussion is a two-way process, Rafe. It doesn't mean trading a few words before we do what you intended in the first place. It's supposed to improve our response, not delay it.'

Fair enough. She had a point. And Rafe couldn't deny that he'd acted out of instinct, a wish to protect her, rather than strictly logically. He pulled his T-shirt back over his head.

'I'll admit I should have waited for Adil and Mushan. But if *you* were thinking logically and reasonably, what prompted you to come out with them?'

Mel's cheeks reddened slightly. 'Irritation.'

Now they were getting somewhere. Somewhere that felt as if it might allow for some acknowledgement of concern for each other, although Rafe would hold out as long as he could before he gave in to that.

'All right, then.' Maybe now was a good time to leave and let Mel think about that. He turned and she caught his arm.

'No, it's not all right. I didn't act very sensibly, and neither did you. If we're going to work together, then I think we'd better come to a more rational arrangement, don't you? Because I'm not just going to follow your lead in everything.'

He could see why that grated with Mel. Practically speaking, he understood the weather conditions better than she did, and what to look out for. But she wasn't the kind of woman who just waited for a man to tell her what to do. Just as he wasn't the kind of man who'd put a woman in danger. Rafe felt his anger subside as rational thought took hold.

'Nor should you. You were right to challenge me.'

Her gaze searched his face. In this moment, he wanted her approval more than he wanted anything.

'Maybe I didn't do it in quite the right way.'

'So let's start again, shall we? We're partners in this, and we make a joint response to everything.'

'You mean…discuss things first?' Mel wasn't going to let him wriggle out of this with a set of vague promises. She saw his hesitation and leaned forward towards him. The scent of roses alone was enough to break him.

'Yeah. Fair enough, we'll discuss.' Just as long as the discussion didn't include how he was beginning to feel about her. He hadn't allowed himself to feel this way since Annu died, and he wasn't allowing it now. But whatever it was that made Mel so fascinating to him paid no heed to what he did and didn't allow.

'Deal?' She held out her hand, and he took it. Small and soft, and yet with a determined grip.

'Yeah. Deal.'

CHAPTER SEVEN

THEY WERE GETTING SOMEWHERE. At least Rafe didn't seem to be about to rush off and try any more feats of daring, although it was difficult to see what feats might present themselves since everything seemed to be very much under control. When a call came through for a non-urgent visit to one of the guest rooms, he clearly felt that going together was an acceptable level of risk.

No one was getting very much sleep, and there was a small group in the bar who seemed intent on drinking the night away. Rafe grinned when Mel frowned up at him.

'The cocktails don't have any alcohol in them. Mr Manike announced that drinks were on the house tonight, but if you look you'll see the optics behind the bar are all empty. He knows it's not a good idea to have anyone getting drunk.'

'They look as if they're well on their way...'

Another raucous round of laughter echoed across the otherwise empty bar.

'Power of suggestion. They're sitting in a bar, drinking something. If something happens they'll sober up pretty quickly.'

'Fair enough. When this is over I'll be ordering a single malt Scotch and savouring every sip of it.'

Rafe nodded. 'I might just join you. They have a good choice of single malts here.'

That would be something to look forward to. Mel had assumed that as soon as the danger from the storm had passed she wouldn't see Rafe for dust, but perhaps he'd stay for one leisurely drink in the sunshine. Before wheeling his sea plane out of its shelter and taking off to fly somewhere else.

They made their way upstairs, to Mr and Mrs Denby's room. The retired couple were on the holiday of a lifetime, and Mr Manike had reported that Mrs Denby was becoming very distressed by the noise and clatter of the storm.

'She won't stop crying.' Mr Denby was looking a little overwhelmed himself when he opened the door to their room. 'Have you got something you can give her to make her sleep?'

'Let's go and have a chat with her.' Rafe smiled breezily and Mel followed him into the room.

Mrs Denby was sitting in one of the armchairs, her arms hugged around her. Every time a gust of wind hit the shutters outside the windows she jumped, tears issuing from her eyes. Mel knelt down beside her, taking her hand.

'Hello there. I'm Mel.'

'Terri. You're the doctor?'

'Yes, that's right. We came to see how you were doing.'

'Oh, dear...' Terri dissolved into tears, and Mel felt Rafe press a paper handkerchief into her hand. 'This is so awful...'

'Yes, it's pretty loud, isn't it? But we're quite safe here.'

Terri gave Mel a disbelieving look. 'Are you sure?'

'Absolutely. This hotel's fully prepared for weather like this.'

One of the perks of being a doctor was that people tended to take your word for things. Mel had about as much experience of structural engineering as the next person, but Terri brightened a little at her assurance.

'There's a lizard in the room.' Terri pointed to a shadowy corner, where a small gecko clung to the wall. Sand-coloured, with dark markings along its back, the creature wasn't much longer than Mel's middle finger.

Rafe took a couple of steps towards the creature, careful not to frighten it. 'We can get rid of that for you.'

'Yes. It could bite or…anything.' Terri waved her hand in the direction of the gecko, which ignored her suggestions completely, staying motionless on the wall.

'You agree that a gecko-catching mission's in order, Dr Murphy?' Rafe's eyes flashed with humour.

'Absolutely. I'm looking forward to watching you try, Dr Davenport.' All of the geckos that Mel had seen during her short stay on the island had been shy creatures which darted out of sight as soon as she took a step towards them.

'I'll just be a moment.' Rafe grinned, leaving the room.

Mel took the precaution of taking Terri's pulse and checking her blood pressure while he was gone. Both very slightly elevated, but what was really wrong with her was that she was scared. In Mel's experience, a few well chosen words and something to do would be a lot more effective than sedatives, and Terri would be much better able to deal with her experience afterwards.

'I'm interested in seeing how he does with the gecko.' Mel smiled at Terri and got a smile back. When Rafe returned, holding a net with a long handle, Terri turned towards him to watch and Mel shot him a smile.

He knew that this had turned into a bit of light relief for Terri and maybe his first lunge with the net wasn't entirely in earnest. The gecko skittered across the wall, coming to a halt and regarding Rafe warily through its large bulging eyes, seemingly ready to race for cover again. But this time Rafe was too quick for it, dropping the net over it and carefully detaching it from the wall.

Terri smiled, clapping her hands together. 'Well done… Be careful though, it might be poisonous.'

'It's harmless. Probably come inside to get out of the storm.' Rafe grinned at Terri. 'I'll find somewhere for it where it won't bother you any more.'

'Thank you. I'd really rather it wasn't anywhere near me.' Terri was beginning to look a great deal better, and hardly jumped when a loud crash sounded from outside.

'I'll take it away right now.'

Half an hour later, she found Rafe in the doctors' ready room, staring at a glass tank which he'd clearly done a bit of work to convert into a comfortable home, with a large bowl of water, some fruit slices and a couple of small, leafy branches. The gecko was motionless on one of the twigs, staring back at him.

'How's Terri?' He didn't look up.

'She's fine. I took her and her husband down to the lounge, where Mr Manike's organised a quiz and some card games. There are plenty of the staff around to lift the mood if needed, and they'll keep an eye on her.'

'Great. Better than sedatives.' He turned, looking at her speculatively.

'Yes, much. Working through things takes a bit longer but it's a lot more effective.' Mel sat down next to him on the bed, looking into the glass tank.

She took a deep breath. 'I've got something to say… About working together.' If she committed herself then she couldn't back out when it came to the point of actually saying the words.

'Yeah?'

Mel swallowed hard. What if telling Rafe that she suffered from an anxiety disorder made him see her differently? He never hesitated and how could his adventurous spirit ever really understand? He might make allowances for her to get them both through the storm, but suddenly she wanted a lot more than that.

The silence was killing her. Suddenly, Rafe smiled.

'We could just close our eyes and jump…'

'You'd like that, wouldn't you.' She smiled back at him.

'Wouldn't you?'

So she was an adventurer too. Suddenly the words seemed easier.

'This morning, outside the medical suite, when I was surrounded by all those people... I had an anxiety reaction and I froze.'

He nodded thoughtfully. 'What happened to you didn't strike me as a reaction to what was going on around you.'

He'd hit the nail right on the head. Anxiety wasn't a response to the real world, it was a response to her own internal world. One where she was stripped of the resources that she'd built up around her to safeguard her life.

'Yes... It's an anxiety disorder. It doesn't mean that I can't deal with what's going on here, Rafe. But I thought you needed to know because...if we're going to work together then we need to know each other's weaknesses.'

'In my experience people with anxiety disorders are very far from weak. They struggle with very real obstacles and symptoms.' He pursed his lips. 'But you're a doctor, Mel. You know this, don't you?'

She knew it. Sometimes she got a little tired of saying it. 'People can think differently.'

His lip curled. 'They'd be the people who

would laugh in your face if you suggested that it was possible to snap out of a broken leg.'

'I imagine so.'

'And you think I'm one of them? That I'd consider this a weakness and it would affect the way I work with you?'

Maybe she had. Rafe was a complex, compelling man and she couldn't help caring what he thought of her. She'd listened too well to her fears and misjudged him.

'That would be very wrong of me, wouldn't it.'

'I'm glad you think so.' He shot her an intoxicating smile, laying his hand on his heart. 'I would have been mortally wounded if you'd got the wrong idea about me.'

'Stop it, Rafe. I'm sorry, okay? You're the one who's been testing me all day.' She couldn't help returning his smile.

'That's how I know for sure that you're a tough cookie and a good doctor. Someone who'll be great in a crisis.'

'So you're not going to apologise for that? I could have tested you out, but I didn't.'

He made out that the words were hard to say, but his eyes were bright with humour. 'I'm sorry. Okay?'

Yes. Suddenly everything was okay. Even the crash of thunder seemed to have receded into the distance, and they were safe and protected here. Mel leaned back on her elbows on the bed, stretching her legs out in front of her to ease the slight ache of fatigue in her back.

'You want to talk about it?' Rafe was obviously tired too and had flopped backwards onto the bed, staring at the ceiling. But yes... Mel did want to talk about it.

'Nothing much to say. You know how it is, bringing a child up on your own.' Maybe she should let him sleep. Let them both sleep, while they could.

'I was never on my own. I had a great deal of support from Annu's family. And I was already qualified, so I didn't have to study as well.' He was still alert and seemed to want to listen.

'I couldn't have done it without my family. And, to be honest, Amy's father leaving was the beginning of everything getting better, although it didn't seem much like it at the time.'

'Not the one for you then.'

Mel shook her head. 'I'd known Michael since I was sixteen. Teenage crush. We decided to go to the same university, and the first year was great. We had a good time. Then I got pregnant. Amy was the best mistake I ever made. The best I ever will make.'

Rafe chuckled. 'Yeah, I get you there. Ash was one of the best things that Annu and I ever did.'

He'd had a good marriage. Mel envied him

that, even though he'd lost his wife. 'Michael and I didn't do much else that was good. He seemed okay about it when I told him I was pregnant, and said we'd get married when the baby was born.'

'He wanted to wait?'

In retrospect, that had been the first warning sign. 'He said that I'd want to look my best at the wedding.'

Rafe shot her an incredulous look. 'I've always rather liked that pregnancy glow... But that's not really the point, is it?'

'No, it's not the point at all. He was making excuses. Michael always liked to be at the centre of things, and he didn't see why my being pregnant should deprive him of anything that he enjoyed. I'd decided to stay at university until the end of the academic year and it was tiring. He started going out on his own and... I never really knew when he'd be coming back.'

'So you had to shoulder all of the responsibility in the relationship.'

She liked that Rafe seemed to always see the realities of a situation. She could now. 'He reckoned that just being there was enough and I was lucky that he was standing by me. I was young and I bought that line. The first time I really questioned it was when I had Amy. Michael was off somewhere doing something, I don't know what, and I couldn't contact him.'

'That's unforgivable.' Rafe's tone was suddenly ice-cold.

'Well, I managed it somehow. Largely because by that time I didn't feel that I was worth a great deal more. I thought that things would get better, but they didn't. I wasn't losing the baby weight fast enough and I was no fun any more.'

'Ah. So everything was your fault then?'

'That was his line, and I bought it. I'd taken a year off from my studies and money was very tight. He spent most of what we had, staying out nights and coming home with lame excuses. I thought that if I could just read the situation a little better, and be what he wanted, then things would be okay. I was trying to make it work for Amy's sake.'

She'd been so wrong. Mel could see that now. And she could see how the anxiety had grown, watching Michael and trying to anticipate his fickle moods.

Rafe had sat up straight, his frame tense and rigid in the silence.

'Say something, Rafe...'

He turned to face her. 'Something you don't already know for yourself? Not sure I can come up with anything.'

'Say it anyway.' Mel wanted to hear it. On his lips, the words seemed more powerful.

'What he did was cruel and irresponsible. The unforgivable part of it is that he made you believe that it was your fault and not his.' Rafe paused, his gaze searching her face. 'Did you forgive him?'

He understood what had really hurt her. And Rafe had allowed for her muddled emotions, in a way that Mel hadn't always been able to.

'A week before Amy's first birthday, Michael just didn't come back. There was no word from him, but a couple of days later I collected Amy from the nursery on my way back from lectures and found that he'd taken most of his clothes. When Mum and Dad came for Amy's birthday party they saw what had happened and packed all of our things up, squashed them into the car and took us home. I still remember going to bed that night, feeling that I had someone to look after me…'

That simple feeling had been so strong that it got to her, even now. Mel felt herself choking on the emotion of it all. And Rafe didn't flinch away from it, he just hung on in there and waited.

'Mum and Dad really stepped up for me. I'm the eldest of five, and they took care of Amy along with my youngest brother and sister. I could continue with my studies and I was able to come home and spend some time with her, instead of doing housework and cooking. I was getting panic attacks by that time. I had been ever since Amy was born and I worried about her constantly, but things seemed to be getting better. Then Michael called. Apparently the grass wasn't greener on the other side, and he wanted us back together again.'

Rafe was having a hard time keeping silent. She could see it on his face. But still he said nothing.

'I said that I could forgive him but that we had to discuss how things might change. He told me I'd always had unrealistic expectations of him, and put the phone down.'

'So you un-forgave him?' Rafe finally gave in, and added something of his own expectations to the story.

'Not right then. He wouldn't come to Mum and Dad's house to see Amy because he said it was a hostile environment for him, and every now and then he'd call me and ask me to meet up so that he could see her. Sometimes he'd turn up, and sometimes not. He'd talk about getting back together, but there was always something I'd done which gave him a reason not to. Then one day, when Amy was four, we were waiting in the coffee shop for him and Amy started to cry. He was terribly late, and she was bored and wanted to go home. Michael turned up, took one look at her and asked me how on earth he could be expected to care for a kid who cried all the time.'

It had been another moment of clarity. Another turning point. Mel let it hang in the air for a moment, because it had cut through all of Michael's excuses.

'I'd been seeing someone for the panic attacks, and I went to see my therapist the following week and told her that I was never going to let him treat Amy the way he'd treated me.' Mel smiled at the memory. 'That was when I un-forgave him for good.'

'And your daughter?' Rafe seemed to know instinctively what the next big challenge had been.

'Amy has a right to know Michael if she wants to, but it's my job to protect her. I went to see a family lawyer and told him that I wanted him to help me work out a set of ground rules that were centred around Amy's well-being. Meeting up in safe places for her rather than what Michael said were safe places for him, for instance.'

Rafe nodded, his brow creasing. 'It's a difficult thing to balance.'

'As it turned out there wasn't much balancing

to do.' Mel shrugged. 'Michael didn't like the implication that he was the second most important person in the room, and simply disappeared from our lives. About the only thing that Amy remembers about him is that she couldn't rely on him, and when she was old enough to make her own decisions she made it quite clear that she had no interest in pursuing any relationship with him. When she got married she asked my dad to give her away. It was one of the best parts of the day, seeing how proud he was when he walked her down the aisle.'

'And what about you? You have all you want?'

No one ever questioned that now. Maybe here, without the trappings of her life around her, it was possible to see a little more clearly.

'The anxiety hasn't ever quite left me, as you saw today, but I have coping mechanisms and it's under control. I have peace, and the life that I want.'

Rafe nodded. 'One of the best things about getting older. You work your way around to accepting the way you are, without trying to be perfect. Saves a lot of time, doesn't it.'

'Yes, it seems to.' Mel wondered what it was that Rafe had to accept about himself. Maybe she could ask…

'No Mr Right?'

Mel thought about her answer for a moment.

She wanted to tell Rafe a little bit more than she probably should. Perhaps that was one more thing she could accept about herself.

'No. Mum and Dad always encouraged me to go out with my friends and to meet people, but once bitten, twice shy, I guess.' That made her sound unreachable and some part of her wanted Rafe to reach her. 'I was persuaded that I might try dating again when Amy was in her teens, but nothing ever came of it. It was all very polite and discreet.' So discreet sometimes that Mel had hardly known herself that she was in a relationship.

The difference between that and the way Rafe challenged her made her catch her breath. The glint in his eye was never particularly polite or discreet, and it reminded her that it was the risk, the meeting of two minds that didn't necessarily agree and two people who could work that out that made any relationship exciting enough to hold on to. Even if holding on was more than she'd ever been able to handle.

'So you're unforgiven too?' He interrupted her reverie with an awkward question.

'What makes you say that? My therapist oversaw a rather long process of forgiving myself.'

'Once bitten, twice shy implies that you think all men are like your ex-partner.'

'No! I don't think that at all. It's obviously not the case.'

'Then logically…maybe it's you?'

No one could challenge her the way that Rafe did. And engaging with that challenge made her feel stronger and not weaker. Mel wasn't at all sure how that worked.

'I don't know. There are always two sides to a relationship, and I accepted Michael's behaviour far too easily…' Mel shook her head. 'I think that accepting happiness is a thing too, whatever shape it comes in.'

It was Rafe's turn to think about an idea now. Maybe his wife's death had made it difficult for him to see happiness in terms of anything other than what he'd lost.

'Maybe… You might be right.' He rubbed his hand over his face, as if trying to knock his thoughts back into place.

He was tired, and so was she. It had been a good talk, and Mel was grateful to him for listening. Even more grateful that he'd accepted and understood, even if her therapist had drilled it into her that she never needed to be grateful just to be accepted.

'I suppose we should try to get some rest.'

'Yeah.' Rafe stretched his arms, catching his breath at just the point when Mel reckoned the stitches on his left arm would start to pull. 'The hotel staff will wake us if we're needed.'

'How long have you been up?' It occurred to Mel that he'd probably already made the flight from Male' this morning, before she'd even finished breakfast.

'Since…early.' He suppressed a yawn. 'A couple of hours and I'll be fine.'

He did seem suddenly very tired. Maybe the efforts of the day, or maybe just that their conversation had gone as far as it could. Or perhaps just force of habit from their years spent training. A junior doctor took whatever sleep they could get, whenever they could get it.

'I'll go and look in on Zeena. Get some sleep.'

She left him alone in the doctors' ready room, returning to find that Rafe seemed to have just flopped over onto the bed and fallen asleep as soon as his head hit the pillow, his legs still hanging over the side of the bed. Mel unlaced his boots, pulling them off, and he stirred a little as she lifted his legs up onto the bed. By the time she'd covered him with a sheet though, he was fast asleep again.

She took off her own boots and lay down on the bed on the other side of the room. Probably best not to get undressed, as she might be hitting the ground running.

It seemed strange to close her eyes, knowing

that there was someone else in the room. But the soft, regular sound of Rafe's breathing, almost drowned out by the storm and punctuated by the gecko's soft chirping, was a powerful tranquilliser. Her own breaths seemed to mirror his as she started to doze.

CHAPTER EIGHT

THE QUIET BUT insistent knocking penetrated his dreams. Rafe sat upright, fighting with the sheet that covered him. He didn't remember lying down on the bed, or taking off his boots, but he must have done so. He definitely didn't remember the sheet…

He stumbled in the direction of the door, stubbing his toe on the way. By the time he pulled it open, he was awake.

'Is the baby coming?'

Haroon gave him a broad, excited smile. 'We think so.'

'Go back to your wife then. We'll be right there.'

Rafe switched the light on and saw Mel sleeping soundly, despite the crash of thunder and the sound of rain outside. For a moment he hesitated. She was lying on top of the bedcovers, still wearing the jeans and T-shirt she'd had on during the evening. She looked peaceful, and so very beautiful.

He reached out, his fingers brushing against her shoulder, and she didn't stir. So he tried shaking her and the result was much the same as his own awakening. Only when Mel sat up straight in her bed, her hair sticking out at several different angles, her cheek still flushed from the pillow, she looked utterly lovely.

'Uh… Baby…?'

'Yep.'

'Don't just stand there then. Get moving, Rafe…'

The mad scramble slowed to a brisk walk as they made their way towards Zeena's room, Mel tying her hair back as she went and looking irresistible in pink scrubs. Zeena's contractions seemed to be coming regularly now and two of her neighbours, obviously chosen to be her birth partners, were already with her. Haroon was hovering nervously by the door.

Mel stepped forward, the smile on her face giving no clue that she'd been fast asleep two minutes ago.

'Would you like Haroon to stay a little longer?'

Zeena shook her head, pressing her lips together in pain. 'No… No, tell him to go…'

'Rafe?' Mel looked up at him and he ushered Haroon from the room. A little cluster of men were waiting for him by the door of the medical suite, and Rafe promised to come and fetch him as soon as there was any news.

When he returned, Mel had washed her hands and was tying a surgical apron around her waist. Zeena had her hand clamped across her mouth to stop herself from crying out when the contractions came.

'Hey, Zeena. It's okay to let it out.'

'I don't want Haroon to…worry…'

'He'll be fine, he's out of earshot. And this is your time, Zeena. I want you to breathe the way your midwife taught you and give me a yell whenever you want to. It'll help, won't it?' Mel smiled at the women with Zeena, who both nodded in agreement.

Mel did everything that was needed, leaving Rafe to monitor the baby's heartbeat and Zeena's vital signs. It was more than just medicine, though. The atmosphere in the room was loving and encouraging, three women helping another to bring a new life into the world. Three hours later, at four in the morning, Zeena's baby son was born.

Rafe had been present at many births since that of his son. But the only thing that could compare with this was the feeling of holding his own child for the first time. It was obvious that Mel's approach centred around each mother's individual needs, and she had made this birth into an affirmation of life, a positive and moving experience.

As Zeena's baby was delivered there were no more words. Mel signalled to Rafe to fetch Haroon and before the cord was cut the lights were dimmed and the new father took his son in his arms. The first human sound that the child would hear was his father, whispering the call to prayer into his right ear. Mel had remembered that too, and respected Zeena and Haroon's religious traditions.

Watching Haroon with his son in his arms brought tears to Rafe's eyes. Not for the wife he'd lost, or the son that he loved so much. These were thankful tears. He hadn't thought that he would experience this feeling again, but somehow Mel had created an atmosphere in the room that had touched everyone there.

She attended to Zeena, suggesting that Rafe might take some photographs of the baby for the proud parents. Then Mel took a few photos of her own, and they left the young couple alone with their baby.

'Nicely done.' Rafe grinned at her as they walked together back up the corridor. 'No one noticed that you had any concerns.'

'I'm rather hoping that I don't. What do you think?' Mel handed him the phone, opening the door of the doctors' ready room.

She'd zoomed in on the tiny baby's face, and Rafe studied the photograph carefully. Then swiped to the next photograph. Mel had got a better angle and it was immediately clear what was bothering her.

'Looks like a cataract. In his left eye...' Rafe enlarged the image on the small screen. 'I can't see if there's one in the right.'

That would make a difference. Most often, both eyes were affected if a baby was born with cataracts due to illness or hereditary factors. Just one eye meant that the cause was more likely to be some kind of injury in the womb. Mel nodded.

'I looked carefully but I didn't see one. That doesn't mean there isn't one there, and the left eye is just more noticeable. We'll have to investigate.'

And that meant alerting the new parents to the idea that their baby might have a problem. Always a difficult conversation, but Rafe reckoned that if anyone was equal to it then Mel was.

'I have a good friend in London who's an eye specialist, and maybe she can give us some pointers.' She'd taken her phone from her pocket and was staring at it. 'I've only got one bar, though…'

'Try her.' Rafe glanced at his own phone. 'I've only got one bar too, so that's no better. The phone mast is probably still up and working. It's just that the storm's making reception difficult.'

She nodded, flipping open a messaging app and typing furiously. She pressed *send* and then sent another couple of messages, enclosing the photographs she'd taken. 'It looks as if they've been sent. It'll be past ten in the evening in London so I might have to wait until the morning, and hope we have some reception then.'

Mel sat on the bed, putting her phone down. It seemed so easy, natural even, to sit down next to her.

'We'll give them half an hour together. Then we can go in and do some more checks on the baby.' He stared straight ahead, clasping his hands together. What he really wanted to do was give Mel a hug.

'Yeah. I've done all of the initial checks, but they don't know that. We can say it's routine…' He felt the mattress move as her phone buzzed and Mel jumped. She snatched up her phone, stabbing at the *answer call* button.

'Maddie…?'

The image on the screen was breaking up a

little, but it was good enough. Rafe could see a blonde woman in a red sleeveless dress.

'Mel… You caught me at a dinner party. I thought you were meant to be on holiday?'

'I am. Well, I was. We have a tropical storm making things a bit more interesting.' Mel smiled. 'This is Dr Rafe Davenport, and we've just delivered a baby.'

Generous. Mel had delivered the baby and he'd largely just watched. But now wasn't the time for any extraneous information, when the connection to a woman who could give them the expertise they needed was so slender. Rafe returned Maddie's wave and smiled.

'So…what medical resources do you have?' Maddie too was ready to get straight down to business, despite her attire.

'We've got good clinic facilities, and we can do just about anything in terms of examination… Maddie…?'

The image on her phone froze and after a few worrying seconds unfroze. 'Okay, I got that. What about hospitals?'

Mel looked at Rafe.

'There are hospitals in Male', which is on the main island, but we can't get there right now because of the storm.'

'They'll have the facilities to deal with infant eye surgery?' Maddie's face froze again in a frown.

'Not necessarily. Leave that with me. I'll get whatever's needed.'

'Good. Okay, Mel, this is what you need to look for. I'm going to message you with a checklist, but I'll tell you now in case it doesn't get through.'

'Wait…' Mel was looking around for a piece of paper, and Rafe got to his feet, fetching a notebook and pen from his own bedside. She nodded an acknowledgement and turned her attention back to the phone. 'Fire away, Maddie.'

Rafe had a few messages to send too. He got to his feet, gesturing to his own phone when Mel looked up momentarily, and retreated to the corridor. No one was around, but he closed the door behind him, standing next to it in the corridor so that Mel wouldn't be interrupted. This might be their only chance of getting some specialist advice for the next few days, and it was precious.

CHAPTER NINE

MADDIE HAD COME through for her. Despite being at a dinner party, she'd managed to find somewhere quiet and called her back. Mel looked at the page of notes in front of her, reading them through.

'Thanks so much, Maddie. I owe you one. Don't forget to call Amy for me, will you?'

'I won't. I'll tell her that you may not be in touch for a while but you're safe and not to worry. I won't mention that you appear to be trapped on a very small tropical island with *the* most gorgeous guy.' Maddie's intent expression was switching back to party mode now that she'd said all she needed to.

'Trapped in a medical centre with no sleep, you mean…'

'Mel! I'm sure you could make the most of it if you tried.' The poor connection couldn't disguise Maddie's smirk. Maybe Mel should take a leaf out of her book and indulge in a few of

the simple pleasures in life, instead of worrying about where they might lead. Rafe's ten-
derness as he'd shown Haroon how to hold his
baby son beat any number of sun loungers and
waving palms.

'Well, the good-looking part will have to wait
until I'm less busy. I'm just hoping that Rafe can
navigate his way through to getting the baby
whatever he needs. He seems to have some in-
fluence here.'

Maddie grinned. 'There you go. Not just
gorgeous, he's a knight in shining armour as
well...'

The screen froze again, and then the call
dropped. That might be just as well. There
wasn't the bandwidth available to accommodate
Mel's thoughts about Rafe. Her phone beeped
and a message from Maddie flashed up on the
screen. Mel waited while it downloaded, and
found it was a checklist that Maddie obviously
kept handy for students and general practitio-
ners.

Thanks, Maddie. Perfect, I appreciate it.

Mel added a couple of kisses to the message
and sent it. Then she sent another.

Re knight in shining armour. You have NO idea...

That would get Maddie's imagination going. She'd wondered aloud whether a tropical holiday retreat might contain any suitable love interests, and it seemed that Mel would at least have a few stories to tell about that when she got home, courtesy of the storm.

Her phone beeped. Maddie had sent a line of smiley faces, along with a comment saying she couldn't wait to hear all about it. Mel sent kisses and an acknowledgement and put the phone back down again. She couldn't wait to find out what might happen with Rafe either, and she still wasn't convinced that any possible outcome would be good. Give in to the obvious chemistry that bubbled between them and then watch him walk away. Or resist it and keep wondering. Neither sounded particularly ideal and whenever she thought about it she felt her heart thump.

The door opened by an inch and she jumped. 'Okay. You can come in.' She'd imagined that Rafe might be waiting somewhere for her to finish the call.

'Got all you needed?' The door swung open.

'Yes, I've got Maddie's checklist and the line stayed up long enough for me to ask her a few questions as well, so I've got a good idea of everything we need to check before we refer the baby on. But if we're right then the baby's going to need hospital treatment. What's the state of play there?'

Rafe's brow creased. 'Maldives has made great strides in making medical treatment available to all of its population, but the very geography of the place poses unique difficulties. There's a scheme which arranges for any Maldivian who needs medical treatment not available here to receive treatment abroad in partner hospitals.'

Mel nodded. 'Any idea what's going to be involved if Zeena's baby needs surgery?'

'I gather that nearly half the surgery for adult cataracts is done abroad.' Rafe shrugged. 'So I imagine that might be the case for the baby. But the hospital I work with in Colombo does this kind of surgery, and is approved as a partner hospital. I've sent a few messages and I'll know more in the morning, but don't worry about that. Whatever Zeena and Haroon need, I'll get it.'

Knight in shining armour. In truth, Rafe didn't look much like one at the moment. He looked tired, and more than a little rumpled. Better, actually, than a knight in shining armour could ever be. As if the smell of soap and a baby, combined with his own warm scent, could be just the thing she wanted to surround her.

'Okay, so medically speaking, there isn't anything that Maddie can suggest right now. If the baby has cataracts then our job is to pick that up, do a little groundwork on what the cause might be, and refer him on to a specialist.'

Rafe nodded. 'So I guess that tonight we could just respond to any questions and let Zeena get some rest. Then speak to them both in the morning?'

'That sounds good.' Mel couldn't help smiling at the way he'd suggested, rather than just told her what they were going to do next. 'Although I'd like to take another look at the baby, just to make absolutely sure that there are no signs of any other underlying condition.'

'Sounds good too.' The smile playing around Rafe's lips told her that the novelty of this joint decision-making process wasn't lost on him either. 'We can just whisk him away for a moment and give him a thorough checkup. That's standard.'

'I agree. Let me just read through Maddie's checklist, so that I don't miss anything.'

He nodded, sitting back down on the bed next to her. It was very difficult to read with him so close and Mel wondered if she should push him away. Find something else for Rafe to do...

Maybe, since he was a king of the jungle, he could think about taking his top off. That would be enormously gratifying. Mel supposed she could use the excuse of wanting to check his stitches, but that would be mixing business with pleasure. She dismissed the thought, trying to focus on the words in front of her.

'Anything else we can agree on while we're about it?'

Yes! Actually, no. The only thing that Mel could think of that they might agree on was going to get her into deep, deep trouble, even if it would give her something to tell Maddie when she got back to London.

'I... Why don't I send you the checklist?' Having him close enough to read over her shoulder meant that she wasn't doing much reading.

'Yeah. Thanks.' There was a note of disappointment in his tone, which matched the sinking feeling in her heart. Mel ignored it, and forwarded the checklist on to him. Then... *then*...just when everything was going so well, and she had herself under control, she made the mistake of looking up at him.

Those eyes. If the king of the jungle had been telling her that he wanted wild sex in any number of different positions, right here in the doctors' ready room, the message couldn't have been much clearer. But there was a trace of the knight in shining armour in the look on his face. As if he would ask for only one touch of her hand, as a mark of her favour.

Mel wondered if he'd ask. Then his gaze dropped to his phone.

No, no, no... If she'd learned one thing in the last twenty-three years, since Michael had left, it was that there was nothing wrong with saying what was on your mind. It was the things that remained unsaid which had power over her, and it was the wrong kind of power.

'It never stops being moving, does it? Seeing a new life come into the world. A new person with so much potential...'

He looked up at her, heat sizzling in his gaze. Maybe he saw the same heat in hers, but Mel guessed that would never be enough for Rafe. He'd never act on an assumption. He needed more than that. She did too. One of the enigmas that accompanied the passing of the years. It became easier to talk about things, but also a bit more necessary.

'It's moving. I thought you handled the whole thing very well.'

'You provided the framework. I felt confident in doing what I felt was right for Zeena.'

He nodded. The silence between them sizzled with electricity, as lightning flashed outside, and Mel instinctively moved closer to him.

'I suppose that the storm adds an intimacy to it all.' Rafe seemed to be going through the whole gamut of reasons why they should feel this way, and carefully avoiding the one thing that would explain all of it.

'Suppose so.'

There were any number of smiling, tactful ways that she could stop this. None of them were going to happen. They'd both gained enough experience of the world to be walking into this with their eyes wide open, and that was what would stop them from going too far. Not self-control, because there was no way that anyone could defend themselves against the melting look in his eyes.

'I'm…um…a bit out of practice with this. But I'd like to ask you something.'

Delicious shivers of anticipation ran down Mel's spine. 'I'd like it very much if you asked me something.'

Rafe smiled. 'We've only known each other for twenty hours. But that seems to be enough to make me want to kiss you.'

'I'd like it very much if you did that as well.'

He hesitated. No, Rafe didn't hesitate about anything once he'd committed himself to an idea. He was showing her that this meant something and it wasn't just a passing whim, which was all good because it wasn't a passing whim for Mel either. Then his fingers touched the side of her face, so gently that they made her shiver.

His lips touched hers in the gentlest, most devastating kiss she'd ever experienced.

It took a moment to gather her senses. Rafe had moved back a little, but he was still gazing into her face. Still there, with no trace of regret for what they'd done.

'Nice.' She reached forward, her fingers brushing the material of his scrubs top. Closing and bunching the material in her grip. 'You want to do that again, as if you mean it?'

'You think I didn't mean it?' His mouth curved at the challenge.

And then, suddenly, there was no question about what Rafe meant, or about what he wanted. When he pulled her close and kissed her, each breath, each heartbeat depended on Rafe's demanding, searching presence.

Even when he pulled away from her he still held her in his thrall. He was staring down at her, naked hunger in his eyes. She'd known him for barely a day, kissed him once and she was his.

That kind of thing just didn't happen. It was something else... Mel couldn't think what, but something. This one kiss had triggered more passion than all of the polite, uncommitted affairs that she'd contented herself with over the years.

A knock sounded on the door and they jumped

apart guiltily. Rafe was on his feet in a second, man of action as ever, striding across the room to open the door. There was a quiet conversation with one of the women who'd been Zeena's birth partners and he turned to Mel.

'She says that Zeena's settling down to sleep now. This might be a good time to check on her vitals and do our post birth checks on the baby?'

Mel nodded. Her mouth wasn't up to words just yet.

'Okay, I'll bring him down to the consulting room and meet you there. When you're ready.'

Mel nodded again and he grinned, walking through the open door before turning as if he'd just forgotten something.

'By the way. I meant it…'

'Yes.' The word came out almost as a squeak, which was unlike her. Mel was always in control of any relationship, and knew when to stop and exactly how to walk away without causing any damage to anyone.

But she was rapidly realising that Rafe was different. He gave her a smiling nod and then turned, closing the door quietly behind him.

Every nerve-ending was tingling. Nothing hurt. Rafe couldn't feel the scrape on his arm any longer and the cut that Mel had stitched for him had stopped throbbing. He felt as if he'd just been struck by lightning and then risen to his feet, the possessor of superpowers.

It was all nonsense, of course. Rafe knew full well that it was possible to fall in love after a first kiss, he'd done so with Annu, but their first kiss had taken considerably longer to get around to. Twenty hours was a different matter. How could you love everything about someone when you knew almost nothing about them?

But the feeling just wouldn't listen to sense. He felt like a man who could defy the usual laws of science, or human psychology, or love, or whatever else was involved in what he and Mel had just done. That kiss was the only true thing, the only absolute that he had to rely on.

Zeena was so dozy now that she hardly responded when he took her blood pressure, opening her eyes only when the cuff tightened on her arm. Haroon was almost asleep too, and Rafe operated the controls on the reclining chair by the bed, telling him to get some rest while his son was being weighed and examined.

While he was waiting for Mel, he flipped through Maddie's notes. Clear and concise, they covered all of the things that an ophthalmic surgeon might want to know from a referring doctor.

'How are you with examining for cataracts?' Mel's voice interrupted his reverie, her soft-soled shoes not making a sound on the tiled floor.

'Fair to middling. In the course of my general practice I've seen quite a few kids with cataracts.'

He couldn't help staring at her. Mel had refixed her hair and was pulling on a disposable apron and gloves, ready to work. Her eyes seemed a little wider and her mouth a little redder. If it was at all possible she was a little more beautiful, and Rafe couldn't help but notice every last thing about her. The way she moved. How she smiled down at the baby in the cradle, her finger gently brushing his cheek.

'That trumps my experience. I tend to concentrate on the mothers.' Mel was somehow managing to look at him without directly returning his gaze. It was a talent he should try to emulate.

'Okay, so you'll hold him while I do the examination?'

She nodded, picking the baby carefully up from his cradle, shushing him and rocking him gently when he started to fret. Rafe took the ophthalmoscope from its case, dimming the lights.

'Okay, little man. Open your eyes for me…' Mel moved the baby into a vertical position against her body, and he saw the shadow of her smile in the darkened room. 'There he goes.'

It was tricky to find the right angle without getting too close to her and in the end Rafe gave up, and found his cheek resting against her shoulder. But Mel didn't seem to mind, and he could see what he needed to see, all thoughts of pleasure banished from his head as he carefully examined the baby, noting all of his observations.

Finally Rafe turned the lamps back up again. He didn't have the heart to tell Mel that she could put the baby back into his cradle now, and she sat down with him still in her arms, his eyes closed again now and his little body snuggled against her chest.

'What did you see?'

'The red reflex definitely shows a cataract in his left eye, and there seems to be a slight reduction in the reflex in the right eye as well.'

'Bilateral, then.' Mel's brow creased. 'Then it's most likely to be either congenital or the result of an infection while in the womb, such as measles or rubella.'

'Could be rubella. There's a lot of work being done to eradicate rubella here, but it's still more common than in England.'

'So the next thing to be done is to check whether Zeena had any infections while she was pregnant. Or whether she or Haroon had cataracts themselves when they were children.'

Rafe nodded. 'Yes, I think it'll be better to do that in the morning, when they've both had some sleep.'

'Agreed. I'll sit with them until the morning...' Mel stifled a yawn, as if the mere mention of it was making her feel tired.

'No. You go and get a few hours' sleep. I'll do it.'

'But you're tired too...' Mel protested and Rafe silenced her with a frown.

'That's not up for discussion. I'm back to my autocratic ways. Put the baby down now and I'll check him over quickly for any signs that there are underlying conditions that might have caused the cataracts.'

'It's unlikely. I don't see any signs of Down's Syndrome.'

'Neither do I. Just roll with it, Mel, and let me check.' Mel's obvious dismay at being sent back to bed to get some much-needed sleep was delightful.

She rolled her eyes. 'Leopards never really change their spots, do they?'

'I wasn't even aware I had spots. I think you'll find most leopards feel much the same.' He gave her a grin as she laid the baby back into the cradle. 'Go on, then. I'll come and wake you at about nine o'clock.'

'Eight. I'll take over and let you get a couple of hours' sleep, and then we'll talk to Zeena and Haroon together.'

'Whatever. Go to bed, Mel.' It was just as well that they were taking turns to sleep, because Rafe wasn't sure that he could go back to the ready room and stay in his own bed if Mel was there, however tired he was. The thought of holding her while they both drifted off to sleep was far too compelling.

CHAPTER TEN

RAFE HAD ALMOST dozed off a couple of times, and his arm was beginning to throb uncomfortably. He'd put off going to wake Mel, but she'd obviously set an alarm for herself because she came to relieve him at ten past eight, looking as fresh as a daisy.

'The storm doesn't seem to be moving away yet...' she whispered to him as he met her in the doorway.

'No, I checked the radio and it'll probably last for the best part of another twenty-four hours. You got some sleep?'

'Yes. Go and do the same.'

He was too tired to argue. Rafe almost stumbled to the ready room, where a feeble grey dawn was doing its best to penetrate the shutters over the windows, and not succeeding all that well. Unlacing his boots and pulling off his clothes, he fell onto the bed, half asleep before his head even hit the pillow.

He woke to the smell of bacon and coffee. Reckoned it must be a mirage, and then sat up straight in bed when he heard Mel clattering around in the small kitchen. As far as he knew, mirages didn't come complete with sound-effects.

'You haven't been switching anything on, have you?' he called in to her.

'No. They've got a barbecue going in the kitchen, and I asked them to make bacon rolls. If you don't like them, I'll eat yours.'

'Nice try. I'd walk many miles for a decent bacon roll.' Rafe realised that he was naked apart from his underwear under the sheet that covered him, and quickly pulled on his jeans and shirt.

'These look at least a nine and a half out of ten. Lightly toasted rolls, and crispy bacon with your choice of condiments. Fresh coffee…' And the scent of roses as he walked into the kitchenette, to find that Mel had set a plate with two bacon rolls out on the small folding table, along with a takeaway cardboard cup of coffee. She snatched up the bag that lay on the counter top, along with her own coffee.

'Where are you going? You're not going to join me?' Rafe stretched his arms, feeling the stitches pull a little.

'No, I've got some doctoring to do. There's

another queue forming outside the consulting room. Join me when you're ready.'

'Okay. Anything serious?'

'Not from the looks of it. Everyone's chatting together quite happily, and when I looked out and asked if they were okay there for a few minutes they all said yes.' Mel flashed him a smile. 'I've got one of the concierges going down the queue and asking everyone what they want to see a doctor about. Zeena's fine and the baby's fine, so you can take your time over brunch.'

It might take him a few minutes longer to get going these days, but Rafe hadn't lost the ability to work through the night, and some sleep and then bacon rolls was a luxury. Mel was already out of the door before he could mention that, and Rafe turned his attention to finding his tooth-brush before his breakfast started to get cold.

Twenty minutes later he was washed and ready to meet the day. He set up in one of the spare patient rooms, helping Mel to cut through the queue of people outside.

She appeared in the doorway, just as his last patient was leaving. 'So. Two cases of indigestion, three sleepless nights and a couple of headaches. I did, however, get a broken toe, which provided rather more mental exercise.'

'I'll raise you a broken toe with a sprained ankle.'

Mel shook her head, grinning. 'No, break-ages trump sprains every time.'

'Torn ligaments? They can take longer to heal...'

She raised her eyebrows. 'Someone's torn a ligament?'

'No, I just wanted to know where they came in the pecking order, in case I do come across one. And, of course, anything that needs stitches has got to rate higher than something that doesn't break the skin.' He gave her his smug-gest look, knowing it would provoke Mel. 'I have stitches.'

'What? They're *my* stitches, I'll have you know!'

'I took a look at them this morning, and it's *my* skin. My body's my own...'

'Oh, no. Not when you're bleeding. That arm belongs to me.'

Rafe chuckled, leaning back in his seat. 'Just turn that around for a moment. What would you say if I told you that any part of your body be-longed to me?'

They were teasing, flirting. Maybe it was a way of keeping that kiss under some measure of control, telling themselves they could handle it. Maybe a way of forgetting that there was still a storm raging outside, or that they'd be talking to Zeena and Haroon about their little boy's eyes soon.

Or maybe they were just enjoying it. Rafe definitely was. Whatever. They had things to do this morning. He took his phone from his pocket, calling up the messages he'd received.

'The doctor who usually covers this area has been in touch. She says that she's spoken with the people I suggested and agrees that transferring the baby over to Colombo is going to be the best option, particularly since the storm's going to be putting extra pressure on the hospitals in Male'. So she's going to try to put things in motion from her end. I've alerted the hospital director, and a few other people who can help with getting them over to Sri Lanka once the storm's lifted, so hopefully there shouldn't be any difficulties there.'

Mel nodded, appearing to forget all about which of them his body belonged to, which was something of a disappointment. He could stand having that conversation with her...

'That's great. Now all we have to do is speak to Zeena and Haroon.'

Telling new parents that there was something wrong with their child was always a difficult conversation. Implying that it was something inherited added a second layer of awkwardness. No one could help their genetic make-up, but people did tend to ascribe blame for such things.

Rafe went through everything coolly and calmly. His positive attitude, which Mel had described to herself as overbearing more than once, was actually something of a bonus. Neither Zeena or Haroon questioned his reassurances that medical science could help their baby, or that the treatment he needed would be available to them.

He asked whether Zeena had fallen ill during her pregnancy, and both parents shook their heads. So Rafe gently introduced the idea that the condition might be inherited. Zeena's previously serene acceptance of the situation crumbled, and tears formed in her eyes. This was just what they'd been trying to avoid.

'We can test your eyes now, to find out if either of you have small cataracts that haven't impacted on your vision. It's good if we know the situation for the sake of other children you'll be having in the future. They can be monitored carefully—' Rafe was being positive and reassuring, but a tear rolled down Zeena's cheek.

Mel squeezed Zeena's hand but before she could say something to comfort her Haroon spoke.

'Zeena, you are my wife and I do not want

you to be tested. If Dr Davenport will be kind enough to perform the test on me, then that is all we need to do.'

'Yes, Haroon. Thank you.'

The silence in the room was broken by a roll of thunder. Rafe sprang to his feet, smiling at Haroon. 'Very well. If that's what you want.'

What? Wait… Then Mel saw it. Rafe wasn't just going along with this. He'd be talking to Haroon when he got him on his own and finding out what was going on. She held her tongue, and Rafe ushered Haroon out of the room.

Zeena had stopped crying now, and was nervously reaching for her baby. Mel lifted the small boy from his crib, delivering him into his mother's arms.

'Now that it's just you and me, Zeena, may I ask you something?'

Zeena was looking at her speculatively, clearly sensing Mel's disquiet. 'Haroon can be a little bossy at times, can't he.'

'Was he telling you that you mustn't be tested? Because that's really up to you.'

Zeena smiled suddenly. 'Did you know divorce is very common here in Maldives?'

'I remember reading something of the sort. Maldives has the highest divorce rate in the world, doesn't it?'

'Yes. My mother was divorced three times,

which is not unusual. My stepfather was not a kind man, and would beat us. Haroon knows this.'

'I'm so sorry that happened to you, Zeena. But I'm not sure what you're telling me.'

'When I married Haroon, he told me that he would be my only husband. That he would always be a loving husband to me and never allow what happened to me to happen to our children. He has kept his promise, but sometimes I am fearful. When Dr Rafe said that there was something wrong with our baby...' Zeena bent, kissing the little boy's forehead.

'I can understand that. I'm fearful too, about things that have hurt me.' Mel thought for a moment. 'So this is Haroon's way of letting you know that he won't leave you? Telling you that you don't need to be tested.'

Zeena nodded.

'But you know that this really isn't a matter of fault. We just want to know what's happened so that your baby can be given the best treatment possible.'

Zeena smiled. 'Haroon knows this and so do I. We learned about genetics in school. I cannot help my fears, though, and I have Haroon to protect me from them.'

'But what happens if Rafe doesn't find any cataracts in Haroon's eyes?'

'Then I will talk to him and he will be persuaded when he sees that I have thought about things and I am no longer afraid. Can you understand this?'

All too well. Mel could understand how much it would have meant to her to have a man who would calm her fears, instead of whipping them up to a fever pitch. Someone who would take care of her and Amy.

'You're telling me that Haroon's a good man, aren't you? And that I'm not to worry about you.'

Zeena nodded. 'Yes. Exactly.'

The wait still seemed interminable, though. Rafe was obviously checking carefully, knowing that this test meant more than just filling in the medical facts. Finally Haroon appeared in the doorway, holding a piece of paper which bore Rafe's handwriting.

He walked over to Zeena, sitting down on the bed. 'Zeena, I am sorry. The doctor has found small cataracts in both my eyes, and it seems I may have passed this condition to our son.'

Zeena nodded. 'Then our son is also lucky, that he will be strong and brave like his father.'

Mel glanced at Rafe, and he gestured a signal that they should go now. She followed him outside, leaving Zeena and Haroon talking quietly together.

'If you're going to give me an earful for not saying something about Zeena's right to make her own medical decisions you'd better do it now.' Rafe had walked to the doctors' ready room, closing the door behind them.

'You were right.'

He raised his eyebrows. 'You never cease to surprise me, Mel.'

'You made a call, based on your knowledge of the area and the fact that you'd be asking Haroon a few relevant questions before you examined him.'

'You were listening at the door, were you?'

'No, I was asking Zeena the same questions and probably getting much the same answers. It turns out that she has her own, very reasonable, fears that stem from her experiences as a child. And that Haroon was reassuring her that things are different now.'

Rafe nodded. 'That's pretty much what he said. So…we're trusting each other now, are we?'

It certainly looked that way. Mel had trusted Rafe to ask the right questions, and he'd trusted her. 'Any problems with that?'

He chuckled. 'Not one. As long as you tell me that you would have come out fighting if you'd found that Haroon was making medical decisions for Zeena that she didn't agree with.'

'What do you reckon, Rafe?' Mel looked up at him, and suddenly found herself caught in his gaze. For all the pretence of being at odds with each other, they had more in common than either of them dared to admit.

'Just checking. A storm like this can get to you in all kinds of ways. I'd hate to think that you were losing your grip.'

'Think again.' Mel looked at the shuttered windows, wishing she could see what was going on outside, if only to reassure herself that all that banging and crashing didn't mean that the whole island was sinking into the sea. 'Although I'll admit that the storm's beginning to get to me.'

'Yeah, me too.' Rafe wiped his hand across his face. 'Shall we try the radio again, see if we can find out what's happening…?'

The news from the radio had been good. The storm was expected to pass in the early hours of tomorrow morning, and blow its fury out over the ocean to the west of the islands. It wasn't quite done with them yet, because when Mel checked her phone there was no signal, and Rafe could get nothing on his either. But Mr Manike had been busy, organising both staff and hotel guests to keep everyone occupied, and that afternoon there was a general atmosphere of quiet camaraderie and the feeling that they were over the worst without any significant damage.

They slept in shifts again, although it wasn't strictly necessary to sit up with Zeena and the baby because they were both doing well. But when Mel felt Rafe's hand on her shoulder, rousing her from sleep, the necessity was all too obvious. Pulling him into the narrow bed to feel his body pressed tight against hers was the first thing she thought about, and she sat up quickly, getting out of bed and grabbing a dressing gown to put on over the long nightshirt she was wearing, before she could act on the impulse.

'It's quiet…' She looked around, almost missing the sound of the wind.

'Yeah. I don't think you really need to get up. Everyone's asleep.'

Everyone but her and Rafe. 'That's okay. Get some sleep. I'll see you in the morning.'

She watched the light filter through the shutters in Zeena's room as dawn broke. Listened to the silence, broken only by steady breathing and a fretful sound from the cot that promised that everyone would be awake in a moment, and that Zeena would get a chance to consolidate her progress in feeding her new baby.

An hour later, she heard the sound of activity. Rafe was obviously up and around, and indulging in what seemed to be an inexhaustible need for action. She slipped out into the corridor and saw that the door to the consulting room was open.

'Shush!' She found Rafe talking intently to Mr Manike. 'We've only just got the baby down to sleep again.'

'Sorry...' Rafe gave her an irrepressible grin and Mr Manike added his own mouthed apology. 'Just deciding whether it's safe to go out and assess the damage.'

Mel closed the door behind her. 'And...?'

'Mr Manike is sending a few scouting parties out first. When they report back, the guests will be advised accordingly.'

Mr Manike nodded. 'One of our first priorities is to see if we can repair the mast, so that we can find out what's happening with regard to the baby that needs medical care.'

That would be good. From the look on Rafe's face, it seemed that he considered it a superlative move. 'I'm going to check the plane out, and then go and see if I can help out with the mast. Want to come?'

There was no real reason why she shouldn't. The baby was feeding well, Zeena's confidence was growing and she was recovering from the birth. It was time to let go a little and let her get into her own rhythm.

'Yes, okay. When are you thinking of going?'

'I'm going to fetch breakfast. Then we can get started.'

Mel's stomach was full and she'd laced her walking boots tightly. Even though it was hot, she wore jeans and a jacket to protect herself from the mess made by the storm, and Rafe had found a pair of thick work gloves for her. He appeared holding a large bottle, which contained the gecko that he'd rescued from Terri's room.

'You're letting her go?' Rafe had assured Mel that the tiny creature was female', but drawn the line at giving her a name, on the basis that they might get too attached. Mel took that to mean that he was getting as attached to the gecko as she was.

Rafe chuckled. 'She's a wild animal, not a pet. Neither of us are going to take her home with us, so yes, I'm letting her go. Sooner is better than later.'

He was right. It was easy to feel that the gecko's smile was the result of some recognition, but that was just the shape of her mouth. And the truth was that they would both be going home soon enough. Mel pulled on her gloves, trying not to think about the realities of their homes being on opposite sides of the world.

It had seemed odd to put sunglasses on with a

jacket and boots, but when they stepped outside she needed them. The sky was a cloudless blue, merging into a sapphire sea. The sun shone and, apart from driftwood and branches piled everywhere, and the rather raggedy appearance of the water cabins, everything seemed surprisingly normal.

'It doesn't seem too bad…' There was a lot of mess and water around, and the outside of the hotel no longer looked as pristine as it had, but there was nothing that couldn't be cleared up.

'Yeah. I hope the plane's not been damaged.' He seemed suddenly intent and purposeful and Mel followed his long strides to a large outhouse. The gecko's bottle was thrust into her hands, and Rafe cleared the branches away from the entrance, taking down the shutters and producing a key from his pocket to unlock the door. He hurried past the neatly stacked marine equipment to the far end of the space.

Rafe walked around the aircraft, checking the bindings that held it in place, and looking underneath the fuselage for any signs of leakage. Then he swung himself up onto the top of the float, opening the door of the cabin and getting inside.

'All right?' Up close, the sea plane seemed rather more exciting than it had at a distance.

Or maybe it was Rafe who seemed more exciting, his movements so sure and graceful now.

'Yeah, she looks fine. Want to come up and take a look?'

Yes, but the cabin seemed a little cramped. It would be better to stay in the open air with Rafe. They'd already found out what happened as a result of having been thrown together.

'I'd love to later. But the mast...'

Rafe nodded. 'Yeah, you're right. First things first. I'm rather hoping I have a few messages.'

He locked the door of the outhouse, putting the shutter back in place. Taking the jar from her, he indicated some rising ground to the left, saying that was the easiest route to the mobile phone mast which towered above the island. Then he set off in that direction.

Rafe was still a fast walker. And he still preferred to walk in a straight line instead of taking the path, but that didn't seem quite so counterintuitive at the moment, since the path had disappeared under piles of leaves and broken branches. The ground sloped gently upwards and Mel was out of breath before they were even halfway there. Suddenly he stopped.

'This looks like a good place.'

It didn't actually look any different to any of the other places they'd walked past. Was this a trace of consideration for her, tempering Rafe's desire to get to his destination?

'You think so? I could do with stopping for a minute…'

That was odd too. Admitting her weakness, instead of just gritting her teeth and pushing on.

'Right then…' Rafe seemed to have forgotten all about his assertion that the gecko wasn't a pet, and was grinning at the creature. 'You'll be happy here, doing your own thing.'

He stooped, laying the bottle on its side and taking the stopper out. 'Keep your eye on her. She'll take a minute to find her way out, but when she goes, she'll move fast.'

They watched, both bending over the bottle and waiting. The gecko slowly seemed to get the idea, nosing her way towards the neck of the bottle and pausing, seeming to sniff the air. Then she was off like a flash, with only a small disturbance of the undergrowth to track her path.

'Bye… Take care of yourself.' Mel straightened up, waving after the creature.

'She's where she ought to be.'

'I know. Look after them, love them the best you can, then let them go.' Mel was still a little sore from having done that with Amy so recently.

'Yeah. I still miss Ash, running into my bedroom and jumping up and down on the bed to wake me up.' Rafe turned the corners of his mouth down. 'That's a while ago now.'

'You never quite lose it, do you? That feeling that you want them to be six years old again.'

'No.' Rafe seemed lost in the past for a moment, but when he looked down at her he was right back in the here and now. 'Probably best not to dwell.'

'Mm-hm. No more dwelling.' She looked at the rough ground, sloping gently upwards between them and the mast. 'We've still some way to go.'

Rafe held out his hand, almost bashfully. And, almost apologetically, Mel took it.

It was hard going, through undergrowth that was still wet and had been ravaged by the storm. Once she almost slipped, grabbing hold of Rafe tightly as he steadied her. But soon they were in a circle of cleared ground, the mast looming above their heads. They walked towards a small building which must house the generator and electrical equipment associated with the mast, and where a group of men were talking.

'Dr Davenport.' One of them grinned at him. 'You want your phone working again?'

Rafe nodded. 'Yeah, I'm expecting a few messages. What's the prognosis?'

'Everything's good. But the antennas have

blown down in the storm.' The man indicated a flat, rectangular antenna, which was lying on the ground next to them, and two more which seemed to be lodged in the struts, halfway down the mast.

'So it's just a matter of fixing them back up?' Rafe shadowed his eyes, looking up. 'You have safety harnesses?'

'Yes, of course. We're drawing lots to see who will go.'

Mel kept her eyes fixed on the ground at her feet. She knew exactly what was coming next.

'Well, count me in.' Rafe turned to Mel. 'I'll bet the view's spectacular up there.'

Was he *asking* her? It was difficult to tell, and Mel suspected that Rafe wasn't going to be dissuaded from climbing the mast. It actually didn't look that difficult. In the centre of the network of struts was a ladder with a circular safety cage around it, running right to the top.

'I imagine so. Getting up there looks pretty straightforward.' It was difficult to inject any enthusiasm into her words.

'Right then.' He produced his phone from his pocket. 'Keep an eye on this, will you? Hopefully, we should start receiving messages when the antennas are back in place.'

As she watched the men get into their safety harnesses and go through the safety procedures,

Mel couldn't help a flutter of anxiety for Rafe. What if something broke? If one thing broke, that wouldn't be too bad, but three things breaking simultaneously would send him hurtling to the ground.

Or what if the tower had been weakened by the storm, and just fell over? She walked across to one of the four large feet, planted on slabs of concrete, the huge metal fixings that held them down bigger than the length of her foot. Surely they would hold?

The problem was that she just didn't know. She couldn't measure the odds or assess probabilities, and so fear was beginning to tear at her heart. Maybe it would be best if she went and sat down at the edge of the clearing, so that Rafe wouldn't notice how apprehensive she was.

'Hey.' She jumped as she heard his voice behind her. Mel composed herself and turned to face him.

'Hi. All ready·to go?'

'Yeah. The structure's solid, and it's safe to climb. These guys wouldn't be going up there if they thought otherwise.'

He saw straight through her. Mel nodded.

'Two will be going halfway, to retrieve the antennas that are wedged in the structure. That's actually the trickiest part, and I'll be doing the easy bit and going to the top with a fourth man.

The antennas will be hauled up to the top on cables, and then we'll fix them.' He showed her the two large clips attached to his harness. 'All the while, we'll be using these to make sure we don't fall.'

'Okay. Good, thanks.' She was feeling calmer now. The first best option was for him to stay with his feet on the ground, but that wasn't going to happen, and so the second best was for him to just do it, while she stayed at the bottom and pretended it wasn't happening.

Rafe hesitated. 'Why don't you go and stand with the others at the bottom? They can do with all the help they can get to haul the antennas back up. You might even get a cup of tea.'

He was involving her. And suddenly Mel felt equal to the task of watching him go.

'Okay...yes, okay. I may as well make the tea. They're busy.'

Rafe gave her a melting smile. 'I'm sure they'll appreciate that.'

CHAPTER ELEVEN

IT WAS ODD. Or maybe it wasn't odd at all. Rafe's first instinct had been that there was a job to be done and that he wanted to help with it. That was always his first instinct. But when he'd seen Mel walking away to the edge of the clearing she'd suddenly become his only priority.

He'd worked and he'd built a life. But the only person who'd made him think twice about stepping forward to take on each difficult task ahead was Mel.

He climbed halfway up the mast, stopping for a rest as had been agreed. Rafe looked down and saw Mel, standing with the other men, sipping tea. By some instinct, she seemed to realise that he was watching her and she looked up and waved.

'No looking down.' The man climbing with him gave the smiling advice, and Rafe nodded.

He waved back to Mel and then turned his attention to the top of the mast. It seemed to sparkle in the sun even more brilliantly because he knew that Mel was on the ground, waiting for him.

Mel had insisted on making the tea, and waited with the others. The two antennas were retrieved and examined, pronounced a little battered but good enough for use and then fixed to a pulley to be sent up to the top of the mast. Mel took her work gloves from her pocket, hauling on the cable with the work crew.

Rafe and the man with him were working steadily and deliberately. The first antenna was fixed and everyone took their phones out of their pockets.

'Nothing?'

Nothing. Everyone shook their heads and waited.

Rafe and the other man were working separately now, each fixing an antenna to the top of the mast. There was a pause while they connected them, everyone staring upwards.

'I have two bars...'

'I have three!'

Mel took her phone and Rafe's out of her pocket. They were both vibrating, messages pinging in one after the other. She turned, smiling to the foreman of the work crew.

'I've got messages.'

'Good. Very good…' He began to wave to the men at the top of the tower, yelling at the top of his voice. 'We have messages!'

It was a long climb back down to the bottom of the tower, and Rafe and the other man stopped halfway to rest, as they'd done on the way up. Mel checked his phone, seeing a whole list of messages on the screen, and then put it back into her pocket, turning her attention to her own messages.

He reached the ground, disconnecting his harness and walking swiftly towards her. 'So it worked…'

'Yes, you have lots of messages.' She handed his phone to him and he disengaged the lock screen. Someone handed him a cup of tea and they stood in the sunshine, both scrolling through the all-important news that had been sent.

'Maddie got the photos I sent, of Haroon's and the baby's eyes…'

'Yeah? What does she say?' Rafe looked up from his phone.

'The baby definitely has all the signs of cataracts and he should be referred to a specialist straight away. It's a bit more difficult to tell with Haroon but she says that she'd be wanting to investigate further on the evidence of what we've described.'

'Great. That's very useful. Can you send it on to me and I'll forward it to the doctor in Male' who's arranging the treatment?' Rafe paused for a moment, reading through something. 'It looks as if the transfer to Colombo will be authorised. My colleagues there have managed to expedite that.'

'Good. Will you be going with Zeena and Haroon, back to Colombo?' Mel felt her heart beat a little faster. This was all good news but it meant that she was losing Rafe.

'Um…' He was scanning another message and then he looked up, grinning at her. 'Apparently not. I've been asked to stay here for a while and set up a medical hub for the surrounding islands. Anyone who's been hurt in the storm, or in its aftermath. The hospital in Colombo will be sending someone over to accompany Haroon and Zeena as soon as the transfer's been authorised.'

'Really?' Mel couldn't conceal her delight.

'Yes, resources are stretched at the moment and the doctor who usually covers this area is needed elsewhere. The sea plane means that I can get around, and the hotel's clinic facilities are ideal.' He looked up at her. 'Are you in?'

'Yes! I'm in.'

'You don't want to relax and finish your hol-

iday?' He was teasing now. He knew full well
that she didn't.

'Be quiet, Rafe. This is much more interesting than a holiday.'

He grinned, typing a reply on his phone. It
buzzed again, as if someone had been waiting
for his reply. 'Looks as if we're up already. They
want me to visit one of the neighbouring islands
as soon as I can.'

They made a hurried farewell to the work crew,
who were packing up their things ready to go
back to the hotel. Rafe was making no conces-
sions in his pace this time, and Mel was glad
of his guiding hand, and the downward slope
between them and the hotel.

His first task was to speak to Mr Manike.
Then everything else started to fall into place.
Work parties were quickly arranged and Mel
saw guests, along with staff, helping to push
the sea plane back into the water under Rafe's
careful supervision, then bringing out the
metal-edged boxes of medical supplies that he'd
brought with him.

Rafe hurriedly showered, washing off the
grime from his foray up the phone mast, and
Mel climbed into the seat next to him. An hour
had passed since Rafe had received the message, and they were ready to go. A group con-

gregated on the beach to watch the sea plane taxi across the water and as it gathered speed plumes of spray rose on either side, obscuring Mel's view. Then suddenly they were in the air.

'Oh! It's beautiful!' She couldn't help catching her breath at the serene blue of the ocean and the paler ring of shallow water around the island. The white beach surrounding a heart of green.

'Yeah.' Rafe seemed a little tight-lipped, concentrating on the task ahead of them. That, above everything else, even her own fears of the unknown, made her suspect that it would be a challenge.

The sea plane flew low and when Rafe circled their small island destination to find a good landing area the difference was obvious. There was a sprawling hotel on one side of the island, and from the air she could see that it hadn't fared as well as their own. There was evidence of damage, and the people who had straggled out onto the beach seemed dejected and aimless. Rafe landed the plane, taxiing carefully to a small jetty where they could disembark and unload whatever medical supplies they needed.

Rafe and Mr Manike's careful preparations for the storm became a great deal clearer to Mel now. These people had no support, the hotel was a shambles and no one seemed to be doing anything about it. It was a far cry from the quiet optimism that she'd seen after the storm on Nadulu.

Rafe turned to her. 'Mel, I'm going to say something that might not make you feel any better.' The look on his face told her that it definitely wouldn't.

'Okay, fire away. Whatever's happened here can't be worse than what's in my head at the moment.'

His lips twitched in a smile. 'I've already got that message. I need you to be careful and stay watchful. I'll be issuing a few orders, and it would be great if you could tell me your objections in private.'

'I get it. These people need direction, and it's nothing personal.'

'Yeah. Exactly.'

She nodded, undoing her seat belt, and Rafe got out of the cockpit and helped her across the float and onto dry land. The crowd milled around them and she saw that several people had untreated cuts on their faces and arms. Some were shouting.

'Can we have some quiet?' Rafe's voice rose above the rest, and demanded acquiescence. 'I'm Dr Davenport and this is Dr Murphy. Is the manager here?'

'Yes!' A smiling man in a casual white shirt

and trousers stepped forward. 'I'm the manager.' Very different from Mr Manike. Mel was beginning to appreciate his formal, rather authoritarian manner.

'Right. I need these people back in a safe place in the hotel, and two of your staff here with the plane. We'll also want space for triage and treatment of patients.'

The manager looked around and, before he could decide what to do first, Rafe had already beckoned to two young men, who had been trying to marshal and calm the others.

'Will you stay right here, please, and make sure that no one touches the plane?'

'Yes, Doctor.' One of the men almost sprang to attention, and he and his colleague moved to a spot between the plane and the crowd, shooing everyone back.

'Everyone move quietly back to the hotel. You'll be given further instructions there.' The press of the crowd became less insistent as people started to turn and walk back up the beach.

'I have the perfect place for you.' The manager was obviously falling into line too. 'Follow me.'

The crowd parted to let them through and Mel stayed close to Rafe as he marched up the beach towards the hotel. She nudged him and he looked down at her.

'Your bossy side is surprisingly useful at times.'

Rafe grimaced. 'I thought you were going to give me a break?'

'This *is* me giving you a break.'

'Ah. Good to know.' She felt his fingers brush the back of her hand. They were going to get through this chaos.

They'd worked through a whole roomful of people with minor injuries, mostly cuts from flying glass, and returned to Nadulu with a full complement of passengers. Dave had a cut on his leg that had become infected, and he was already running a slight fever. Mel had administered intravenous antibiotics and decided that the medical suite was the best place for him for a couple of days.

Izzy had torn at both of their hearts. A seven-year-old girl who had been blown off her feet when a branch crashed through the window of her parents' hotel suite. She'd escaped with only minor cuts but had broken her wrist and been in severe pain since yesterday. Rafe had applied a splint and asked if she'd like a ride on a sea plane, and the little girl had managed to give him a smile.

Izzy's parents and Dave's wife had filled the other seats for the short flight. Hotel staff were waiting for them, and helped transfer Izzy and Dave to beds in the medical suite. Izzy's mother had looked around her and burst into tears of relief.

Two more patients had arrived by boat from one of the other islands, battered and bruised after falls during the storm. Mr Manike had settled them into beds in the doctors' ready room, and rather apologetically told Mel that one of the female' concierges had gathered her luggage together and transferred it to a premier suite on the top floor of the hotel.

'Mr Manike, you're a wonder. Keeping all of our patients in one place is perfect, thank you.'

'All part of my job, Dr Murphy. Nothing is too good for our doctors.' Mr Manike gifted her with a rare smile, which made it all the more special, and walked away.

She saw Rafe heading towards the consulting room and hurried after him, hoping that he knew where the key was for the medicines fridge that he'd brought with him when he'd first arrived on the island. Mel slumped down into the chair behind the desk.

'Those poor people, Rafe. I could hardly bear to leave them.'

'Yeah. But we did the best we could. We triaged and then treated everyone in order of need. There are boats on the way from Male' to take everyone off the island this evening.' Rafe had put in an urgent call with the travel company that ran the hotel, insisting on medical grounds that the evacuation take place today.

'I know, but I wish we could have done more.'

'Hey. How many cuts did you stitch?'

'I've lost count.' Rafe's apparent obsession with helping to fix window shutters seemed entirely reasonable to Mel now that she'd seen the results of badly fixed ones at first hand.

'Too many to count is a respectable total. You can never do as much as you want in these situations.'

'I'm just realising how lucky I was to be here, where things were better organised.'

Rafe nodded. 'Makes all the difference. Mr Manike can take a lot of credit for that, although I don't suppose he will.' Rafe had been fiddling with his key-ring and finally managed to detach the key for the medicines fridge. 'There you go.'

'Thanks. You couldn't put it back on the key-ring and then take it off again, could you? I'm not sure that I can stand up right now.'

He chuckled, bending down to wrap his arms around her and pull her to her feet. Mel was wide awake now. All it took was the brush of his cheek against hers.

'Right. Thanks.' She pulled her scrubs top straight. 'I suppose I'd better get on.'

There was still more to do. Mel had left Dave's wound open to allow the infection to drain and it needed careful monitoring, even though Dave had expressed the opinion that a little walking around would probably do wonders. His wife Beverley had had the last word on the matter, telling him briskly that he was to stay exactly where he was and do as he was told. Mel knew an ally when she found one, and had carefully gone through everything that Beverley should bring to her attention.

Izzy was a joy. Mel had found Rafe in her room and, while he finished talking to her parents, Izzy had proudly showed off the temporary cast on her arm, whispering to Mel that she could sign her name next to Doctor Rafe's.

Their other patients, two young men, looked as if they'd been beaten up, after having ventured out of their hotel during the storm. One had been slammed against a sea wall and the other had been trapped under a tree that had been uprooted by the gale. The hotel's first aiders had given them a thorough going-over when they'd arrived and they'd been under their watchful eyes ever since. Rafe examined them both and confirmed that there were no broken bones, which was a minor miracle considering the number of bruises they both had.

'Guys, I'm not going to ask what you thought

you were doing.' Rafe shot them both a pained look. 'But would it be safe to say you'll think twice about going out in a tropical storm in future?'

'Yeah, definitely.' Robbie was the more cheerful of the two. 'There were six of us and we had this bet—'

'No, don't tell me.' Rafe held up his hand. 'Seriously, I don't want to know anything other than you're not going to do it again.'

Robbie grinned. 'Fair do's, chief. Never again, eh, Brian?'

His friend stirred in his bed, wincing as he did so. 'Are you kidding, mate? Of course never again.'

Rafe walked out of the room and closed the door behind him. Then he leaned against the wall, closing his eyes.

'What?' Perhaps he'd finally ground to a halt after a day's unremitting work and couldn't find the energy to take another step.

'I went out. In a tropical storm. On my own.'

Mel laughed. 'Oh, and you want to know whether I think you're as much of an idiot as those two in there?'

'Don't beat about the bush. Just tell me.'

'Yes, Rafe. You're an idiot. But you had very good reasons. You were trying to keep everyone together and out of danger. I didn't really realise how important that was until today. And you were quite right when you said that there were only two doctors and it didn't make sense for us both to take the risk.'

'Okay.' He put his hand against his chest, his eyes still closed. 'That didn't hurt too much.'

'There was a trace of machismo there, though. That thing of wanting to be the one that goes, so the woman doesn't have to do it.'

'That hurts.' He opened his eyes. 'I trust there was a bit more than just a trace.'

'Oh, so you admit it?' Mel put her hands on her hips.

'Yeah. Beat me up for it if you like. I'm far too tired to feel it.'

He was incorrigible. Not at all the kind of guy that Mel would usually have fallen for... But then those discreet relationships with friends seemed unbearably polite now. The kind of man who would never challenge her and make her feel the way Michael had. But challenge was what she lived for in most other parts of her life and Rafe was beginning to show her that she was equal to that challenge in a relationship as well.

'Come to my room.'

He raised his eyebrows. 'So you can beat me up in private? Or is that a proposition?'

Mel smiled. One thing about Rafe, she never

had to worry about him not saying what was on his mind and that meant she didn't have to stop and wonder what the most tactful way to say anything was.

'Neither. I'm far too tired. But I could watch a sunset and there's no one else around to do it with.' Or to understand. All of the frustration and all of the little victories they'd won today.

Rafe thought for a moment. 'Sounds good. I just need to hand over to the hotel first aider first. I'll see you up there?'

'All right. See you there.'

She took the lift to the top floor of the hotel, checking the room number on the card in her hand. It would be okay to leave the door open for Rafe. He wouldn't be long. The hotel's first aiders were both very competent and knew when they should call for a doctor.

The sun was sinking towards the sea, already sending golden ripples through a backdrop of blue. And this was just the place to watch it, big floor-to-ceiling windows and a couple of very comfortable-looking sofas. The coffee table in between them held a large display of flowers and a bowl full of tropical fruits. Mel looked at the note which accompanied the flowers.

To Dr Murphy. With heartfelt thanks, J Manike

Mel smiled. Less was most definitely more where Mr Manike was concerned. She walked over to the folding doors which separated the bedroom part of the suite from the living area and found that the same floor-to-ceiling windows gave the same stupendous view. All of her things had been arranged neatly and her empty suitcase stowed away next to the wardrobe. In the adjoining bathroom there was a gift box containing scented soaps and moisturisers. Mel squirted a dab of the handcream onto her hand and it was thick and luxurious.

'Hey. This is *nice*.' Rafe's voice floated through from the living space.

'Isn't it? I should be wearing a beautiful dress before I even think about watching the sunset.'

'You don't need the dress. And scrubs are a much more telling badge of achievement.'

Rafe said the nicest things. As if they were just matters of fact and not compliments at all. It made her feel that she didn't need to thank him for making her feel good, as if it was a pleasure she didn't wholly deserve.

'What's that?' She nodded towards the bottle and two heavy cut-glass tumblers that he was holding.

'You said that you'd be ordering a single malt Scotch when the storm was over. I guess it's over now, even if there is a lot more for both of us to do.' He put the bottle down on the table and Mel squinted at the label.

'You have good taste. That's expensive Scotch.'

'Blame Mr Manike. I found it in my room instead of flowers and fruit.'

'No, you don't get away with that. I blame *you* for remembering.' Mel sat down on the sofa and Rafe took the opposite one, pouring a splash of Scotch into each of the glasses.

'Ice?' he enquired innocently.

'I'm not watering this down.' Mel picked up her glass. 'What shall we drink to?'

Rafe considered the question for a moment. 'Getting through?'

'Is that *all* we did? Just get through?'

He chuckled. 'Getting through together then. That was a bit more challenging at times.'

Mel chinked her glass against his 'Getting through together.'

His gaze held hers in an embrace as they drank. Mel leaned back on the sofa, closing her eyes to try and keep that image in her head for as long as possible.

'I think I'm too tired to watch the whole sunset.'

'Yeah. Me too...'

CHAPTER TWELVE

MEL WOKE UP. The sea was sparkling in the early morning sunlight, and she was lying comfortably on the sofa. This was a great sofa, she'd have to get one like it at home. These peaceful, bright mornings were something she'd like to take home with her as well. The scent of flowers and the sound of Rafe's breathing…

What?

She rubbed her eyes, looking across at the other sofa. Rafe was fast asleep, his lips curved in a slight smile as if his dreams were good ones. And she couldn't remember for the life of her how she'd got here. She'd been sipping Scotch…

That wasn't to blame. Most of her drink was still in the glass on the table. Her sneakers were under the coffee table but she recalled slipping them off when she'd sat down. And she had her socks on. No one had sex in their socks, did they?

'Rafe! Wake up!' Her tone must have been more urgent than she'd intended because he sat up suddenly.

'What is it?'

'Um…nothing. You were just asleep. And it's morning now.' Mel gave him an embarrassed look.

'Ah. Yeah, okay. Thanks for noticing.' He looked around, clearly wondering the same as she had. 'Yesterday was a tiring day, wasn't it?'

'Yes, it was. I didn't stir all night.'

'Me neither.' He frowned. 'Actually, I did. I woke up and ate one of your rambutans.' He nodded apologetically towards the fruit bowl.

'That's okay. Help yourself.' This was just excruciating. It would have been much better if they *had* had sex last night. At least the endorphins would help with the morning after.

'Right then. Well, I'd better be going.' He looked at his watch. 'Six o'clock. Early breakfast in an hour?'

'Yes, I'll look forward to it. Don't forget your Scotch…' Rafe was already halfway towards the door.

'Uh…hold onto it, will you? We can try again with the sunset…'

'Try again?'

He stopped suddenly, turning around. 'There's going to be another one this evening and I'd like to watch it with you. Maybe we could do it without the scrubs and the exhaustion this time.'

Mel's heart began to beat a little faster. 'You mean a date?' The words slipped out before she could bite her tongue. She should have just said *yes* and left it there.

'We could call it that…' He turned and suddenly all of Rafe's charm and adventurous certainty seemed to drain away. This terrified him too.

'Mel, I'm not asking you for a pleasant evening that may or may not turn into a very pleasant night. Will you come on a date with me?'

There was a world of difference. She'd spent a lot of years convincing herself that a nice meal followed by satisfying sex that didn't leave you wanting to go back for more was enough. This was uncertain and delicious, and didn't have a sell-by date stamped on the wrapper.

'I…haven't been on a date for a while.'

'Me neither. Are you okay with the idea?'

No. Not even slightly okay. But she wanted it.

'If you are…?'

He thought for a moment. All of Rafe's defences were down and he was taking this seriously. 'Yes. I'm definitely okay with it.'

'Me too.'

He gave a nod, as if his throat was as dry as hers and words were just as impossible. Then he turned, his pace brisk again as he walked out of the room.

Mel flopped back onto the sofa, looking up at the ceiling. The storm had been a hard taskmaster, constantly pushing them together and pulling them apart. But she'd already proved that she was a lot tougher than the things that life could throw at her. There would be another sunset and she and Rafe would be there to watch it.

By the time they met in the restaurant for breakfast Mel had stood under the shower for long enough to calm herself. Rafe obviously had as well because he was smiling and relaxed, ready to talk through the things that needed to be done today.

Their patients were their first concern. Mr Manike had extended an invitation to both Dave and Izzy's families to stay at the hotel until they were fully recovered and ready to travel. Brian and Robbie were bruised and aching but well enough to return to their hotel and Rafe would fly them back there this afternoon. Zeena and Haroon would be leaving for Male', to catch a flight to Colombo later this morning.

They spent an hour with the couple, discussing what would happen next. Zeena and Haroon seemed even closer, even more in love with their baby son if that was at all possible. Mel's own experience after Amy's birth was so different, and it was touching to see them together. As they were going through the notes, making sure that they were all in order before they were handed over to the doctors in Colombo, Rafe's phone buzzed.

He picked up his phone and smiled. 'Looks as if we have a visitor...'

Mel followed him out of the hotel and down to the beach, wondering how *they* could have a visitor when their circle of friends and acquaintances was entirely separate. A white speedboat was nosing its way into dock, against the newly swept jetty, and Rafe started forward suddenly as a young man climbed out.

Even from this distance, she could see who it was. Their visitor was familiar from the photographs that Rafe had shown her and he had his father's easy way of moving. The two men met on the jetty, giving each other an unashamed hug, warmth of a kind that you couldn't manufacture. Then they began to stroll towards her.

Ash. Rafe was always happy to see his son, that went without saying. The slight reservation that nagged at the back of his mind was over something that hadn't even happened and probably never would.

That wasn't the point. When Ash had been

old enough to ask, Rafe hadn't denied that he'd had a few 'women friends' since Annu had died. As Ash had got older he'd assumed that might involve sex, in the same way that Rafe had assumed that when his son went away for the weekend with a girlfriend they might or might not be sleeping in separate rooms. But the one thing that Ash knew for sure, and had always known, was that there had never been anyone who could replace his mother.

Mel had asked Rafe to kiss her as if he'd meant it. And he had. He'd *really* meant it, and that was a first for him. It made very little difference that they hadn't done anything more, because Ash was smart enough to see that Mel was different. Rafe wasn't sure how he might feel about that.

'It's been a great help to have another doctor here.' Mel was hanging back, watching them as they strolled towards her, and Rafe decided that telling Ash who she was would be the most natural thing to do.

'You've not been running her too ragged, have you, Dad?' Ash grinned at him.

There was no good answer to that. 'Not as far as I'm aware.'

'Okay. Don't tell me then.' Ash grinned at him, striding forward to shake Mel's outstretched hand and introduce himself. She was smiling and a little pink-cheeked in the sunshine, as if she too felt the awkwardness of the situation.

'So what brings you here, Ash?' Mel asked.

'I'm here to collect the family whose new baby has cataracts. The hospital said they'd send someone, and I volunteered. Thought I'd check up on what Dad was up to while I was here.'

Mel looked as taken aback by the thought as Rafe was, and he decided to change the subject before she felt impelled to answer.

'I imagine that Zeena and Haroon will be spending much of their time at the hospital, but if they need somewhere to stay you've got the keys to my guest house, haven't you?'

'Yes, I'll sort that out. I hear you're staying here for a while, island-hopping.'

Rafe smiled at his son. 'Do me a favour and try to make it sound as if I'm doing *some* work, or I'll be answering to the hospital administrator when I get back.'

'Unlikely, Dad. She told me to remind you to leave a little something for the other doctors in the area to do.'

They strolled to the medical suite together, chatting amiably. When Ash sat down to read the notes, Rafe decided it would be okay to leave him alone with Mel for a few minutes while he got coffee.

When he returned, balancing three cups on a

tray, he heard Ash's voice floating through the open door of the consulting room.

'I'm specialising in surgery. My ambition is to help bring simple surgeries to rural populations in Sri Lanka. We can help change a lot of lives…'

He shouldn't eavesdrop. But he was so proud of Ash. Then Rafe heard Mel's voice.

'That's an admirable goal. I know that progress is being made, but that there's still a lot more to be done.' Mel's tone was interested and encouraging.

'That's right. New techniques are being developed all the time and I really want to be a part of that. Not just a part of it, I want to be on the cutting edge. I know it'll take a lot of hard work…'

Rafe couldn't resist stepping forward, and Ash and Mel both looked up at him at the same time.

'He's not afraid of that.' He gestured towards the file that lay on the desk in front of Ash. 'Read the file. You want to get a good practical solution of how to get specialist help in an isolated situation then it's right there. Along with a few very good examples of the right questions to ask and the right way to answer them.'

Rafe set the tray down, putting Mel's coffee in front of her, and she looked up at him. Just the hint of a smile and the hint of a blush. She waited for Rafe to sit down and then turned to Ash.

'I'm very interested in what you've been saying about your own career. You might find it useful to be in touch with some of my contacts in London. Perhaps I could take your phone number?' She flashed Rafe a querying look and had obviously been waiting for his return before she broached the subject.

Ash hesitated. 'It's kind of you, but I wouldn't want to put you to any trouble.'

Rafe leaned back in his seat, grinning. Mel's contacts would be a good addition to the resources at Ash's disposal. He'd worked hard and gained the respect of the people around him. It was time for him to start spreading his wings.

'If a doctor of Mel's seniority and experience offered to take my number I wouldn't hesitate.'

'You don't need my number, Rafe. I'm sitting right here.' Mel rolled her eyes but looked pleased at the way he'd emphasised the words *seniority* and *experience*.

Ash took the blatant hint and grinned, handing over his phone so that Mel could save the number on hers.

They'd said their goodbyes and Mel had hugged Zeena, planting a kiss on the baby's forehead.

She shepherded the couple along the jetty and Rafe hung back to give them some final time alone.

'Mel's really nice.' Ash was standing beside him, watching her.

'She's a good doctor.'

'Not what I meant, Dad.'

'Yeah. I know.'

His son fell silent for a moment, and Rafe reckoned he'd said enough. He should probably work out exactly what was going on between himself and Mel before he said anything to Ash.

'Dad, I didn't ever get the chance to talk with Mum, but you and the family brought me up to know what her values were, right?'

'Yes. Your mother was a good woman, and she'd be proud of you.'

'I know. I can't speak for her, but I think I understand the way she might have thought. She'd be proud of you too, and want you to be happy.'

Rafe considered the question. 'I'm glad you think so. But I *am* happy with my life, Ash.'

'Happier, then. Look, Dad, I know you loved Mum and that your relationship with her was something special. Having something else that's special doesn't wipe all that out, does it?'

'We're at the stage where you start giving me advice, are we?' Rafe didn't mind that at all, and he'd wanted to hear what Ash had just said, more than he was able to admit.

Ash rolled his eyes in exasperation. 'Dad…!'

'Sorry. I'm listening. I just don't have an answer for you right now.'

'You'll think about it, though? I'm not telling you what to do.' Ash was smiling now. 'But… you know…'

'I know.' Rafe gave his son a hug. 'You're telling me that whatever I do is okay, and I really appreciate that, and that you took the time to say it. Thank you, it was a good talk.'

'Any time, Dad.' Ash looked a little relieved that Rafe had drawn the talk neatly to a close.

'You've got a patient waiting for you. Go and get on the boat.' Rafe grinned, nodding towards Mel, who was holding the baby while the pilot helped Zeena to her seat.

'Yeah. Don't worry, I'll look after them. See you soon…'

Ash hurried away, smiling at Mel as he took the baby from her and got carefully onto the boat. She waved, calling something that was lost in the sound of the engine, and Ash waved back. As the boat drew away, she watched it go and then walked back to Rafe.

'You're right to be proud of him, Rafe. He's impressive.'

Rafe turned, not wanting to watch while the

boat disappeared over the horizon. Goodbyes weren't his thing. 'It was good of you to take his number.'

'My pleasure.'

They started to walk together across the sand to the hotel. Finally Rafe summoned up the courage to ask the question he really wanted to ask.

'So could *I* have your number?'

Mel thought about it for a moment and then smiled. 'Yes. You can have my number.'

CHAPTER THIRTEEN

THEY'D FLOWN TOGETHER AGAIN, taking Robbie and Brian back to their hotel and making sure there was no one else who needed them. Calls to the other four islands that Rafe had been asked to look after produced no other patients, and on the way back Rafe had dipped and wheeled, putting the sea plane through its paces and Mel's heart into her mouth.

Dave and Izzy were both progressing well, and the medical suite suddenly felt very empty. Rafe had disappeared on an errand somewhere, and the sunset was only four hours away. Mel went to the consulting room and opened the condom cupboard, surveying its contents. She wasn't taking anything for granted, but there was no harm in being ready. There were so many difference choices, though…

'You found them, then.' Rafe's voice sounded suspiciously cheery and Mel slammed the cupboard door closed, looking round to find him leaning in the doorway.

'No. I can't think where they've put the plasters.'

'Plasters are over there. That's the condom cupboard.'

'Right. I wanted plasters.' Who was she trying to kid? Rafe didn't look even slightly convinced. 'Okay. How did *you* know that was the condom cupboard?'

'I came across it when I was looking for plasters. They've got a dazzling selection, haven't they?'

Mel sighed, opening the cupboard again. She'd been caught in the act and denying it was only going to be even more embarrassing.

'Yes. It's pretty impressive.' She heard his footsteps and looked around the door to find him standing next to her. Maybe choosing their favourite condom would break the ice that seemed to be forming around her.

'What do you say we forget all about that?' Rafe took her hand, pressing it to his lips, then closed the cupboard door. 'This is something different for both of us.'

'Yes.' Mel's throat felt suddenly dry. A date really was more challenging than any of the other relationship options available.

'Would it help if I said that I don't think I'm

the guy that brings condoms with him on a first date?' He shrugged. 'Not as far as I remember, anyway.'

The panicked feeling lifted suddenly. 'It helps. As far as *I* remember, I appreciate the gesture.'

'You like picnics. And swimming?'

'Yes.'

'Then I'll see you in half an hour.'

'That sounds perfect.' She reached for him, suddenly unable to let him go. 'Are you open to—?'

'Yes.'

She pulled him close and he backed her against the door and kissed her. Great kiss. Then he kissed her again. Even better. More head-swimmingly, heart-stoppingly delicious.

Just as she was about to leave him wanting more, he left her, wanting so much more that she could hardly bear it. She pulled him back, kissing him one more time.

'Half an hour.' He whispered the words against her ear.

'Yes.'

'Don't bring condoms.'

'I wouldn't dream of it.'

This was the first time in Rafe's life that *not* having a packet of condoms on hand had opened up the number of options available. It wasn't that he didn't want to have sex with Mel. He wanted it so much that he was having trouble stopping thinking about it. But it was complicated. They both needed to take their time and be sure of what they were doing.

And this *was* something different. Physical intimacy no longer felt like the betrayal it once had. But becoming involved with someone, the way he was with Mel, was entirely different. His belief that true love could happen only once had been fuelled by the idea that maybe heartbreak would only happen only once as well.

He knew all about risk, how to calculate and minimise it, and Rafe understood the risk involved here. Mel had put her life back together after a disastrous relationship and she had peace now. He'd grieved and then found a way to make his life mean something. They were neither of them perfect, but they'd found a way to live with their imperfections. It didn't sound much, but experience told Rafe that that was one hell of an achievement.

And, on top of all that, they lived on opposite sides of the globe. Compromising with each other was a commitment which wasn't to be taken lightly.

He still wanted her, though. And wanting her made him selfish enough to contemplate the risk. When they met in the reception area of the hotel, packed sandwiches and fruit from the kitchen in the bag slung over his shoulder, she seemed to glow. And when they walked together into the sunshine, Mel sparkled. Rafe wanted her smile, and the scent of roses that she always seemed to carry with her.

Hand in hand, he led her to the place he'd selected for them to swim. A small cove on the other side of the island, which none of the other holidaymakers seemed to have found yet because it was deserted. Ahead of them the sand merged into sea in a wash of colour and behind them a gradient in the land afforded a sense of privacy.

'This is gorgeous!' Mel clapped her hands in delight. She wore a bright sarong over her bathing costume, her hair tied up. Rafe had been concentrating on admiring the curve of her shoulder all the way here.

'I think so.' She *was* gorgeous. 'Shall we swim first?'

She smiled up at him. 'It would be wrong not to.'

This moment was all about a sheer love of life, that feeling of freedom that he always felt when Mel was smiling at him. The breeze against his skin as he took off his shirt, and the feeling of his limbs moving as he broke away from her, running to the massive trunk of a palm tree that bent over the water.

'Rafe!' The note of panic in her voice made him stop, but when he turned she was smiling. 'Tell me you're not going to break your neck.'

'I'm not going to break my neck.' That seemed enough for her and he heard Mel's laughter as he scrambled up the trunk, launching himself into the air in an expression of the joy that life seemed to hold at the moment.

There was a satisfying splash as he hit the water and he saw bright flashes as startled fish shot out of his way. Then he hit the surface, feeling the rush of adrenaline pulse through his body and the sun on his back.

If only she'd let go of her fears and experience these simple pleasures. But what was pleasure to him was an agonising *what if?* to her. He waved, beckoning to her to come into the water.

She hesitated. Rafe could almost see the cogs turning in her head, weighing up all of the possibilities. And then she did it. Mel walked over to the palm, climbing onto its trunk and slowly straightening to stand. Arms out at either side of her, she started to walk slowly out over the water.

'Be careful...'

She wobbled slightly and he caught his breath. At least he'd taken advantage of a few handholds to make his way along the trunk, but Mel's back was completely straight, her steps slow and controlled like a ballerina.

'You're telling *me* to be careful?'

'I couldn't balance like that.' Any minute she was going to go headlong into the water.

'Does that make me more foolhardy than you?' There was a look of intense concentration on her face.

'More accomplished...' More beautiful, more graceful. Maybe a little less willing to hurtle her way through life and just feel the wind in her hair, but he was realising that Mel had nerves of steel.

He watched as she walked carefully, never putting a foot wrong. The pliable trunk bent a little beneath her weight and Rafe found himself trying to solve impossible calculations of angle and height. Then she turned, looking down at the water before she jumped in.

She landed a little way away from him, the water pluming up around her. For a moment he couldn't see her and sudden fear made Rafe strike out towards her. Then Mel's head broke the surface, and she was grinning at him.

'Nice one.' He wanted to draw her a little closer but he didn't dare.

'You want to try it my way?'

'I'm not sure that I could.'

'If you try mine, I'll try yours.'

That was a challenge he couldn't pass up. It had the hint of a lover's dare about it, and Mel's lips held the hint of a lover's reward if he could pass the test.

'You're on.'

He swam back to the beach, pulling himself up onto the trunk and standing. This wasn't as easy as Mel had made it look. Twice he stumbled and stepped down into shallow water, and then he got a little further and splashed down into the water next to her.

'Don't look at your feet. Look at where you're going.' Mel offered the advice and Rafe wondered how that was going to work if he couldn't see where he was putting his feet.

Okay. Try again. This time he reached the end of the trunk and dived into the water. He surfaced to the sound of Mel whooping and clapping her hands above her head.

'Now you…'

She looked speculatively up at the trunk. 'Any advice?'

How on earth did one advise on spontaneity? 'Uh… No, not really. Run with the wind.'

'Okay, that's helpful.' Mel got out of the water and took a tentative run at the trunk. She missed her footing almost immediately and stumbled back onto the sand.

Maybe this wasn't such a good idea after all. She was going to hurt herself if she tried that again. She was far too hesitant and not letting her own instinctive ability to grab at a few handholds take over. Rafe swam back to the beach, but not in time to stop her from jumping up on the trunk and trying another run.

But, moving fast, he was just in time to catch her. She slipped just as she was over the water's edge and Rafe managed to scoop her up before she hit the ground, holding her tightly as his heart beat fast.

'Maybe it's not such a good idea after all.'

'What?' She wriggled free of him. 'You can do it, but I can't?'

'It's not a matter of who's allowed to do what. I don't want you to hurt yourself…'

She was backing away from him now. And then suddenly mischief showed in her face. Mel started to run across the beach.

'No, no, no…' She veered closer to the foot of the palm trunk and he started to run after her. 'Don't do it, Mel.'

He reached forward, just missing one of her flailing arms. She got away from him, describing a wide circle on the beach, her laughter serving only to encourage Rafe in trying to catch her. Before he knew it she was scrambling up the trunk, and he followed her as she sped nimbly along it.

He caught her, just as she reached the point where he'd launched himself into the water. Curling one arm around her waist and hanging onto the broad base of a palm frond with the other, he pulled her close, never caring that they were touching in ways that he'd dreamed of, just feeling the balance of her weight against his.

Mel was laughing, and trying to wriggle free of him. A sudden madness took over, and Rafe let go, holding her against him as he jumped. They hit the water together with an almighty splash, and she was still in his arms as he surfaced.

'I've got you...'

She gave him a bright smile, winding her arms around his neck. 'I thought I had you.'

'Yeah, I guess you do.' All he could think about at the moment was that they had each other. And, if he wasn't very much mistaken, she wanted that as much as he did.

One kiss. It was more of a peck really, but it shook him to the core.

But, in the curious paradox of a first date, wanting more was enough. He took his arm from around her waist and she let him go. The bright prospect of spending time with her seemed to glisten like the sunlight on the water, and that was all that mattered.

They'd had a great time. They'd swum and eaten their picnic. Baked in the sun a little to dry off and then wandered back to the hotel, hand in hand. Rafe had kissed her hand in a quiet gentlemanly touch, the look in his eyes that accompanied it telling her that he'd rather she didn't go to her room alone. Mel would rather not as well, but this relationship was worth spending a little time on, and doing it right.

She sat alone, watching the sunset. Wishing he was there to watch it with her and yet something told her that he'd be watching it too. Alone, but thinking of her. Rafe had been right. It would take time for them both to find the moment when they could finally give themselves to each other. And his willingness to wait, to take nothing less, touched her in a way that no other man had done before.

She smiled as the bright display of amber and red began to spread across the sky.

'I did it…'

She'd been afraid to climb up on the palm trunk, and almost baulked at the idea. But she was even more afraid of going back to a life where anxiety shackled her. She'd learned how to push through the big things, changing jobs, signing the agreement to buy her house, determined to make a good life for Amy and herself. But somewhere along the way she'd neglected the little things. Those simple pleasures, the thrill of making it to the end of the palm trunk and the rush of water against her skin when she'd jumped in became things of great value when she was with Rafe.

She should think about going to bed, to sleep. There would be a lot to do tomorrow and... But she wanted to wait a while and watch the bright array of stars as it appeared in the sky. On a clear night they were so much brighter than they were at home, and she should take this pleasure while she could.

'Ugh. Not again...!'

So it was a comfortable sofa, she'd already established that. Mel hadn't meant to sleep on it for a second night in a row, but she'd been watching the stars. And it had been well worth it, even though her neck was a little stiff.

That eased when she carefully massaged the muscles under the hot water of the shower. When a waiter arrived, with her early morning wake-up call and a large cup of coffee, there was an envelope on the tray.

Mel took a gulp of the coffee, tearing the envelope open and smiling when she saw Rafe's handwriting.

I loved every moment of our date together. May we do it again this evening?

One more pleasure that had been lost. The frisson of anticipation, of not quite knowing what would happen next and allowing Rafe to surprise her. Mel had come to feel that surprise wasn't necessary when it came to relationships.

But she couldn't keep still now. She picked up her coffee, making her way down to the medical suite. Rafe was sitting in the consulting room, writing up notes in a patient folder.

'Yes. I had a wonderful time and I'd love to do it again.' Probably not the most well thought out of replies, but that didn't matter because Rafe's smile told her all she needed to know.

Mel sat down, taking a sip of her coffee and then handing it to him. He turned the cup, drinking from where her lips had touched it, and then handed it back.

'Say…six o'clock?'

'Six is great. Where are we going?'

'Somewhere nice.'

Okay. A surprise then. 'What should I wear?'

He grinned. 'Whatever you like. I have one

decent shirt, which is currently being laundered, so I don't have much choice in the matter.'

'Okay. I have a choice, so I'll think about it.'

'I'll wait to see what you decide on then.' He leaned back in his seat. 'And, meanwhile, we have Izzy and Dave here, and there have been some calls from a couple of the other islands, so I think I'll need to visit. Would you like to come?'

'Yes, I'll come. I want to make sure you'll be back for six.'

The sea plane had touched down at five o'clock. There had been more to do than they'd thought and Mel might have been tempted to sit down and put her feet up, but she was too excited for that. They'd parted in the reception area, Rafe going back to the medical suite to check on Izzy and Dave, and Mel going to her room.

She knew just what she was going to wear. She'd brought a dark blue dress with her that was cool and comfortable, and yet still dressy enough for the evening. The jagged hem was filmy around her ankles and she had one pair of high-heeled sandals to go with it. Mel showered and took time over her hair and make-up, smiling at herself in the mirror. Since Rafe hadn't told her what he had in mind for tonight, there was no need to agonise about whether this was appropriate or not. She could dress to please herself, or to please him if she wanted.

The look on his face when she met him in the reception area told her that this *did* please him, very much. And Rafe had obviously made an effort too, his white shirt and chinos neat and freshly laundered. He whispered a compliment in her ear and she whispered one back, before he led her outside to one of the buggies that guests used for getting around the island.

He took the wide path into the trees, turning into a part of the forest that Mel hadn't seen before. She could see a light glimmering up ahead and when he stopped the buggy she saw steps leading around an enormous trunk and into a pool of light that emanated from the heart of the tree.

'I thought...' He seemed suddenly unsure of himself. 'Since I promised you a sunset, this is the best place to see it from. If you don't want to climb up there we could go somewhere else.'

'It's wonderful, Rafe. However did it survive the storm?'

'The steps and the platform at the top all come apart surprisingly easily. One of the work teams put it all back together again as part of the clean-up operation. I went up there myself last night and checked that they hadn't missed anything.'

Right now, Mel felt she would be safe anywhere if Rafe was with her. 'So you were watching the stars too?'

He chuckled. 'I may have taken a few moments out to do that as well.'

Rafe took her hand and they walked up the spiral steps. At the top, a sturdy platform with rails around the edge and a canopy above their heads. It was lit by lanterns and at the centre of the platform a table was set with a snowy white cloth and covered dishes.

'Oh!' Mel walked to the guard rail. 'You can see some of the other islands from here.'

'You like it?'

'I love it, Rafe. Thank you so much. This is so beautiful.'

He smiled. 'Sorry, can't see it. I have something more beautiful to look at.'

'Stop!' She nudged her elbow against his ribs. 'You've been looking at me all day. This is only ours for tonight.'

All the same, staring at him as he popped the cork of the champagne that was waiting on ice, and while they ate what Mel could only describe as the most luxurious picnic she'd ever seen, did seem even better than the view. Surrounded by the sounds and the scent of the forest, in their own small world. As the sun began to go down, he refilled their glasses and they walked back over to the edge of the platform to watch.

Tonight, it seemed as if even Mother Nature had pulled out all the stops for them. A magnificent sunset that filled the sky and sent shimmers of gold across the sea towards them. Mel leaned in against his chest and felt Rafe's arm around her shoulder.

'There's something I want to say, Mel. The one thing you haven't asked me about…' He fell silent, as if waiting for her permission to speak.

'Say it.' Mel had a good idea what he meant, and she did want to know.

'You've never asked me whether I still love Annu. And the answer is yes, I do and I always will. But that relationship is in my past now and what I feel for you belongs to us alone, no one else. You've helped me to believe that anything and everything is possible.'

'Thank you. I did want to know and… I couldn't have had a better answer. I don't know what's going to happen next, and I'm still afraid. But I want to be with you more than both of those things.'

He nodded, turning towards her. 'That's how I feel too. Maybe we could take one day at a time, and find out where it all leads?'

'Yes. That sounds like a good plan, Rafe.'

He kissed her. Softly at first, and then as if

he really meant it. They held each other tight as the sunset covered the sky with brilliant colour. As it faded in the sky he led her down the steps to the ground.

The evening had started off at an exquisitely leisurely pace, but now they couldn't wait. When they got to Mel's room Rafe kicked the door closed behind them, taking her into his arms and kissing her.

They stumbled together into the bedroom.

'I have condoms,' Mel gasped as he kissed her again. 'I thought that was okay for a second date...'

'So did I.' He started to pull the zip at the back of her dress, and it fell from her shoulders.

'So, so glad we don't have to go all the way downstairs...' She shivered in the warmth of his gaze.

'Marvellous thing, forethought...' Rafe tore off his shirt, embracing her again.

Her dress fell to the floor at her ankles. Rafe stripped off her underwear and then the rest of his clothes. She felt her back hit the mattress and his body covered hers, strong and unyielding. He smelled of the sun and the forest.

'You're sure?'

He knew she was. But Mel knew that he needed her to say it. The thought that one word from her could let loose something momentous was exquisite.

'I'm sure, Rafe. Are you?'

'Beyond sure…'

One more moment of exquisite stillness. They both wanted the same thing, but there was no rush now, no danger of it slipping away. The one thing stronger than physical pleasure, the knowledge that tonight wasn't just about sexual satisfaction and had everything to do with the look in Rafe's eyes, made her shiver at the lightest touch of his fingers.

He felt it too. When she brushed a kiss against his lips he let out a groan. Each action provoked a deliciously intense overreaction. Rafe's gaze held her tight, in the most erotic of embraces. He saw her. She saw him.

Unable to wait any longer, she took his hand, guiding it downwards. Felt him gently pushing her legs apart, his fingers probing and arousing, making certain she was ready. Mel was *so* ready. And then she realised that no one could ever be completely ready for something like this. He pushed inside her and something seemed to ignite. Rafe moved again, and intense feeling washed over her, completely out of control.

'Mel…?' He hadn't expected this either, but she wrapped her legs around his hips, begging him not to stop. Rafe knew just what to do. He held her tightly, thrusting again, and she cried out. She felt the beginnings of something building between them, something that she couldn't have slowed down even if she'd wanted to. Then, like a bolt of lightning out of a clear blue sky, she came, her body arching and shaking uncontrollably. She felt Rafe's body stiffen against hers and knew that he was sharing these long, exquisite moments of release with her.

It was a while before she could let him go, the moments measured by their pounding hearts. When she finally loosened her arms from around his neck he lifted his weight from her, rolling over onto his back and holding her against his chest.

'Maybe I need to work on my tim ng...' He sounded almost apologetic.

'Your timing is wonderful. I was ready for everything and you gave me everyth ng.'

He pulled her close, kissing the top of her head. 'I was hoping to give you everything for a little longer.'

'I don't think that would have felt so good...' Doubt crept through the corners of her mind. Maybe Rafe hadn't experienced what she had. The sudden, unyielding passion that wouldn't be moulded or prolonged, in just that same way that an explosion couldn't be contained.

'It was exquisite. Amazing. You felt it too?'

She leaned over to kiss him. 'From my head to my toes. One whole night rolled up into the most incredible feeling...'

He chuckled. 'A whole night? You're sure about that?'

'I'm not sure about anything. I'm just waiting to see what happens next.'

'Me too. Since we didn't have time for it the first time around, would you like to play a little?'

That should be impossible, after what had just happened between them. But just the thought of it prompted a tingling reaction that told Mel that nothing was impossible.

'I thought you might want to rest a bit.' Mel kissed him. 'You can rest if you want.'

'No, I can't, not when you're kissing me like that. And I want to get to know your body a little better.'

That sounded just delicious. 'Mmm... I'm looking forward to getting better acquainted with yours too...'

CHAPTER FOURTEEN

MEL WAS PROPPED up on one elbow, watching Rafe sleep in the early morning light. Getting to know each other a little better had turned into a delicious, drawn-out conversation, his body speaking to hers in ways that she hadn't felt possible. Talking and making love into the night, until they'd both fallen soundly asleep.

'You're watching me.' Rafe's sleepy voice disturbed her reverie.

'Yes. Do you mind?'

He chuckled, rubbing his hand across his chest. 'I'm not quite sure whether I should be questioning your taste.'

'I have excellent taste.'

He pulled her down, kissing her. 'And you make me feel good.'

She was leaving it all behind. It was just a matter of keeping her nerve, and not looking down. If she did that, she'd only see how far she could fall.

'Shall I order breakfast?'

'Don't you want to be a little more discreet than breakfast for two?'

No, she didn't want to be discreet, or polite or to keep her distance. Mel had done all that and it bored her. She wanted Rafe's passion, the way he didn't care too much what anyone else said, and the way he swept her off her feet.

'Do *you* want to be discreet?' The thought that maybe he wouldn't want to own up to this affair with her snagged suddenly in the corner of her mind. Without that, he could say as many pretty things to her as he liked, there would still be that nagging doubt.

He wrapped his arms around her, kissing the top of her head. 'I would like to climb the mast again this morning. String up a banner saying *Dr Mel Murphy thinks I'm good enough for her.* Would that be okay with you?'

'No, it would not. It's an unnecessary risk and you might fall.'

'Okay...how about sky-writing?'

'No! It's a waste of fuel.'

'True. How about writing it in the sand then? Big letters.'

Mel smiled. 'It'll be gone in a couple of hours, everyone will have been walking all over it.'

'Right then. Breakfast for two. And just in case the waiter doesn't pick up on the signs and go straight back down the kitchen and start spreading rumours, I'll phone down and order a second pot of coffee.'

'Hmm. That should do the trick.' Mel reached for the phone.

Breakfast for two never arrived. Rafe was still in the shower and Mel opened the door to her room, wondering why the waiter was hammering on it so insistently.

'Dr Murphy… I am looking for Dr Davenport, but I cannot find him…'

'Slow down.' She stepped back from the doorway, beckoning the concierge inside. 'Dr Davenport's here. What's happened?'

'One of the outdoor barbecues was damaged by the storm, and no one noticed. The cook has been burned.'

Rafe appeared, dressed in one of the hotel bathrobes, and the concierge's eyebrows shot up. 'You go, Mel. I'll get dressed and be right behind you.'

The flash from the exploding barbecue had singed the cook's eyebrows and he had a burn on his arm, which was thankfully minor, although it would be painful for a couple of days. When she saw that his injuries weren't significant, Mel suggested that Rafe stopped cooling his heels in the medical suite and that he go and find out what had caused the barbecue to flare up so dangerously.

He returned with Mr Manike as Mel was dressing the cook's arm. After solicitous enquiries as to his employee's well-being, Mr Manike took the man off, leaving Mel and Rafe alone.

Rafe's hands and arms were covered in soot and he was leaning in the doorway, trying not to touch anything. Mel had been trying not to distract herself by looking at him.

'Did you find out what happened?'

He nodded. 'Yeah, one of the valves had started to leak. It's one of those accidents that can happen at any time. The barbecues were all covered and checked after the storm.'

'So no one missed anything?'

'No. Mr Manike's obviously not all that pleased, since he does his best to make everything safe and he doesn't want anyone hurt. But he knows he did all he could to prevent it.'

Sometimes you just had to let these things go. It was a lesson that Mel was learning. All of the checks and balances in the world probably wouldn't have averted this. Suddenly Rafe's attitude seemed a great deal more reassuring. He didn't try to quantify all of the things that might go wrong. He went out and got to grips with the cause of a problem and fixed it.

Maybe that was why she couldn't help but feel

safe when she was in his arms. Couldn't help but smile when she saw him rumpled and covered in grime from whatever task he happened to have got himself involved with.

'What?' He spread his arms, looking down to see if he'd got any soot on his clean shirt.

'Nothing. I was just thinking that you're very reassuring.'

He raised his eyebrows. 'That's nice to know, but I thought you found me reckless. I've been working on it.'

He had. Rafe had been telling her what he intended to do next and making decisions with her. She still didn't feel completely at ease with some of the things he did, but Rafe wasn't reckless.

'I've been working on things too. I have a feeling that being ready for anything is a lot more effective than making a list of what everything might include.' She smiled. 'Not that I'm completely convinced yet.'

He smiled. 'You shouldn't be. Lists are good too.'

They were starting to grow together. Learning to accommodate each other's way of doing things, taking the best and leaving what didn't work. Still different, but that didn't seem to grate any more.

And this was a new pleasure. Smiling at him

across a room, the intimacy of last night still humming in her veins. Knowing that it was still a part of him too.

'I guess we've really done it now.' She held his gaze, looking for any sign of regret and saw none.

'Guess we have. I could probably justify taking you to dinner to watch a sunset, but I can't think of any good reason for being in your room first thing in the morning, dressed in a bathrobe.' He shrugged. 'Other than the truth, of course, which I don't have a single regret about.'

She had no regrets either. Maybe a few worries, but that was natural when you were embarking on something new. Mel was beginning to understand that her aim of leaving a lover without any questions in her mind at all had limited her choices. Caring what happened next was one of the things that had made last night so explosive.

'I don't either. And I'm happy if everyone knows.'

He grinned broadly. 'Really? Because we could send a much more obvious message...'

What was he up to now? Mel felt a tingle of excitement as he strode towards her. Soot on his hands, a smear on his brow...

'No! Rafe, no handprints!' She crossed her

arms against her chest, backing away from him, laughing.

'Shh.' He put his finger against his lips, leaving a smudge. 'Anyone might be listening.'

She couldn't resist his teasing. When he reached for her, tracing his fingers against her cheek, she knew he must be leaving evidence of his caress. When he kissed her there would be more.

Who cared? What was soap and water for, anyway?

They'd been working together for over a week now and sleeping together for the last four nights, and it seemed odd to see Rafe flying away alone in the sea plane. But he had islands to visit, and Mel had patients here to deal with.

But when he came back again she could watch him shower. Today there was rather more mud than water streaming off his body, and the soap he was rubbing along his arms was developing a greenish tinge.

'What did doctoring include today then?'

'You're not going to believe a particularly muddy patient?' he enquired and Mel shook her head. 'Blocked water channel.'

'And dirty water means sick people.'

He grinned, nodding. 'Not yet, thankfully.

Call it preventative medicine. What have you been up to?'

'I saw Izzy and her parents off on the boat to Male', along with a letter and the X-rays for her doctor at home. The two patients we brought over here yesterday are much better and I reckon we can discharge them tomorrow. And I went and spoke with Mr Manike this afternoon.'

'Yes? What did he say?'

'It was as we thought. He hasn't been sleeping. He's been doing so much to keep everything running smoothly, during and after the storm, that he just can't switch off at night. We had a long talk and he opened up about some other problems he's been having. He's on the brink of clinical exhaustion.'

'You told him that?'

'I told him that we were both very concerned about him and that he must try to slow down, before he becomes seriously ill. I went through all of the things that can help him, exercise, dietary changes and allowing himself time to wind down as much as possible before he goes to bed. If he still can't sleep I'll prescribe a mild sleeping tablet, but for starters I tried hot chocolate and bridge.'

'Bridge?'

Mel grinned. 'Yes, apparently he's a bridge player. So I rounded up a couple of the guests who play and managed to get him out of his office to make up a foursome. Then I sent him off home with instructions not to come back until tomorrow. Hopefully he'll get a good night's sleep and we can start getting him into a more healthy routine.'

The water was running clear now and Rafe stepped out of the shower. Mel wrapped a towel around his waist, stealing a kiss at the same time.

'Good thinking. Have you played before?'

Mel reckoned that Rafe probably had. His capacity for just rolling up his sleeves and trying things out meant that he'd done a lot of things.

'No. Mr Manike explained all the rules very carefully, but I still ended up losing all my matchsticks and four lychees.'

'Maybe I'll challenge you to a game then.' He tugged at the fastening of her wraparound skirt. 'You could lose that instead of matchsticks and lychees.'

'Careful. I might improve suddenly and you'll be the one losing your shirt.' She tugged at the towel and Rafe grabbed at it.

'I'll take my chances. I might see if Mr Manike's up for a game tomorrow afternoon, to brush up my skills.'

Mel sat down on the side of the bathtub. Rafe was expecting her to leave him alone to dress, but that was one hundred and twenty seconds of pleasure that she wasn't going to get again.

'You don't like me watching you, do you?' She smiled at his hesitation in losing the towel. Rafe had no difficulty with nakedness when he was doing something, showering, swimming, making love. When she drew attention to it by watching him, he became uncharacteristically shy.

'I...don't get the appeal of it.' His hand went to his chest in the diffident gesture he always made when he caught Mel admiring his body.

'But you understand the other things I like so well...'

'That's not the same thing. I have my mind on you then.'

Mel focused on his face, reaching up to stroke his cheek. Passion ignited in his eyes, but that wasn't what she wanted at the moment. She wondered whether she could ask even more of him.

'Let's do something different, Rafe.' She knew that he couldn't resist *that* challenge.

This was hard. They'd undressed and Mel had propelled him into the bedroom, reclining on the opposite side of the huge bed. That was ough for starters, because he wanted to touch her. Then she'd taken the game a little further, and it had suddenly seemed as if it wasn't a game at all.

He'd been getting used to her watching him. Having her tell him everything she liked about his body was unexpectedly difficult. It was a workhorse, a machine. A means to an end that he fuelled regularly and took good care of. But in Mel's eyes he was a work of art, and that didn't sit too easily.

'I don't think I'm vain enough to believe you.'

'I don't think you're honest enough to believe me.'

Rafe couldn't help smiling. Mel's habit of saying what was on her mind was all the more appealing when she was naked. 'Cut to the chase, why don't you? I can think of far more things to say about you.'

She grinned. 'Go on then. I can take it.'

He let his gaze slip over her body. She didn't even flinch. 'You're in amazing shape. You've been working out pretty regularly, haven't you?'

'Yes, I have. I'm gratified you noticed. Makes it suddenly worth the effort.'

Okay. This he could do. 'And you don't dye your hair. You have a few strands of grey, but I really like that.'

'I'll have a few more before long. Grey seems to be all the rage these days.'

'You carry the look well. You carry your

laughter lines well too.' He touched the side of his own eye and thought better of it in case Mel noticed *his* wrinkles.

'Yours give a lot of character to your face.'

Rafe shot her a reproachful look. 'It's my turn, isn't it?'

'Just saying. I can't help noticing these things.'

'I'm noticing that one of the things that makes you so stunningly beautiful is that you're comfortable in your own skin. You know who you are and what you are, and that's an incredibly sexy thing in a woman.'

'That's an amazing compliment, Rafe, thank you.' The slight flush in Mel's cheeks told him that she'd really liked what he'd said, even if he had only spoken the obvious truth.

An obvious truth that might well have some relevance to his own life. He'd run from his grief and, even though he didn't feel its sting any more, he still had the feeling that the passage of time wasn't necessarily a good thing. That leaving the past behind and living for today, meant that he'd lost the youth who had left England and fallen in love with Annu, and he was only just learning to value the man who was falling in love with Mel.

'Mel, can we stop this? I really want to touch you.' He *did* want to touch her, so very badly.

She nodded, her eyes darkening suddenly with desire. 'I can't resist you, Rafe...'

'Do you want to?' It occurred to him that on some level they were both resisting each other. Both realising that the other challenged the hard-won peace they'd found in their lives. He had a full and happy life here in Sri Lanka, and she had the same in England. Different lives, not just different places.

'No, I don't think I do.' Her gaze slowly moved down from his face, and he felt a throb of arousal. Rafe's hand moved instinctively to cover it and then he stopped himself.

'How about a compromise? You can watch me making love to you.'

He moved towards her on the bed and she reached for him. It seemed that she liked the compromise as much as he did.

CHAPTER FIFTEEN

IT HAD BEEN more than two weeks since Rafe had first met Mel. A relationship that had started in conflict and ended in perfect accord. Rafe woke in the bright clear light of early morning. Last night had been electrifying, and his body was still buzzing pleasantly with its memory.

With three days to go before Mel was due to leave and nothing really settled between them, it seemed that the physical was taking charge and showing them what they needed to know. How to beg a little. When to bend and when to break. How wanting something enough meant that it was possible to give up everything and still feel that you'd lost nothing. All of those strange contradictions that only made any sense when you admitted that you were in love.

And, despite his belief that loving and being loved happened just once in a lifetime, and then only if you were lucky, Rafe had to admit that he loved Mel. And that he was pretty darn sure she loved him back. The feeling that love might turn into loss had held him back, and he still didn't want to think about it. But he had to get a grip and hold onto this new and unexpected happiness. He reached for her, wondering if it was at last time to tell her, and found only an empty space in the bed, still warm from where she'd been lying.

The idea swirled in his head. New and precious, like an orb of light that seemed to reach every part of his being. Rafe got out of bed, throwing on his clothes. He knew exactly where Mel would be.

Mel saw him, walking along the beach towards her. Barefooted, his cream-coloured casual trousers rolled up to save the hems from the spray of the sea. Broad-chested, his polo shirt taut in all the right places. Still a little tousled from sleep and the morning breeze. Rafe was everything her heart wanted.

'Good morning.' She waited for him, greeting him with a kiss.

'I missed you.' He put his arm around her shoulders and they began to walk together in the surf. 'Looking for new horizons already?'

She'd been thinking about them. Wondering what they might be, and whether Rafe would be a part of them. The future had seemed incompatible with their hedonistic enjoyment of the moment, but more and more it seemed that there were promises to be made. Those promises had been on the tip of her tongue more than once in the last few days, and she'd seen them in Rafe's eyes too.

'I was considering them.' She still didn't quite know how to put it all into words. Ever since Michael had smashed her horizons to pieces she'd carefully removed them from any man's grasp.

'Me too. I...' He stopped suddenly, taking her hand and raising it to his lips. 'Mel, I can't imagine a time when those horizons don't include you.'

She caught her breath. This was everything she'd been wanting Rafe to say to her, and yet now that he'd said it she was afraid. Maybe fear was a good thing. It sharpened the mind and helped you get things right.

'I can't imagine that either.'

'This is a hard thing for me to ask but...would you consider staying on for a little while? A few weeks. Months maybe, if you could take that amount of time off work.'

Months. Maybe. Disappointment made her pull away from him.

'Rafe, I... I can't do that. I mean I probably could. I'm self-employed and I've deliberately set my work up to be flexible. But how can I spend just weeks with you and then go home again?'

He pressed his lips together, and for once Mel couldn't see what he was thinking. 'I thought… if you came to Colombo with me, then you could see how things work at the hospital there. See my home…'

'And then go back to London?'

'I didn't say that. Then we do whatever we want to do.'

Go with the flow. Swim with the tide. Rafe could allow things to work themselves through without being crippled by anxiety. Mel had learned to live with that, enjoy it even, but now that they were about to take the next step in their relationship her fears resurfaced, hitting her hard. What if she fell back into that downward spiral of anxiety, which would leave Rafe's own adventurous spirit no room to breathe?

'I can't do that, Rafe. I'm sorry. I really need some kind of plan.'

She could see the hurt in his eyes. Feel it in her own heart. And then he backed away from her, shaking his head.

'I'm sorry too, Mel. I love you, and I don't want you to be uncertain about the future. But I need more time and a little more space to come to terms with the idea that committing myself for a second time won't ultimately lead to loss. If you could just trust me…'

'You can't leave it behind, can you? The past…'

'No more than you can. But give it time. I really believe that we can get there.'

Could she accept Rafe's commitment to today, without knowing what the future held? Mel wanted to share his sure belief that the future would take care of itself and that it didn't need to be planned out, but the wash of anxiety at the thought told her that this was a step she couldn't take.

'I know it's a great deal to ask, particularly since we haven't known each other for very long. But how can you believe in something so fully, when you still don't know how and when you're going to do it? If you're going to do it, even.'

'Because…' he shrugged '… I just do. I know that I love you.'

'Then talk to me. We'll both put all of our cards on the table and we'll figure something out. We've worked out how to make decisions together already, and this is just a bigger, harder decision.'

'One that we can make when we're ready. Give it a little time.'

This couldn't be happening. Not like this. Mel

had known it would be hard, but surely it wasn't impossible. Rafe wasn't asking so very much of her, and she wasn't asking much of him. It was just the sting in the scorpion's tail, that neither of them could give what the other asked.

'I can't give you something I don't have, Rafe. I know myself, and I need to know what I'm going to do next. Without that, everything will just spin out of control and I'll let anxiety destroy everything we have.'

His face hardened. 'Then there's only one thing to do. We end it right now.'

The shock stunned Mel into silence for a moment. His quicksilver, impetuous heart didn't know how to stop him from acting, once he knew what he had to do.

Rafe turned and walked away. And Mel couldn't stop him, because she knew in her own heart that he'd done the right thing.

Mel was packed and ready to go. She'd managed to get a last-minute seat on a flight from Male' to Colombo, and when she got there she'd hole up in an airport hotel for a couple of days until her holiday flight back to London. It wasn't going to be the best of journeys, but it was better than being here, on a small island with the man who had broken her heart.

She couldn't even bring herself to hate him

for it. They'd been under pressure and their fears had reared up and smacked them both in the face. And Rafe had put an end to it all, before it could be taken from him. She'd seen the sea plane climb in the sky, and she had no idea where he was going or when he'd be back.

There was only one person she had to say goodbye to. Mr Manike was sitting in his office, and when she knocked and entered he sprang to his feet.

'Dr Murphy.' The formality belied the warmth of his tone. 'What can I do for you?'

'I came to say goodbye, Mr Manike. And to thank you for everything you've done to help keep us safe here. I know it's been a gruelling task.'

Mr Manike smiled. 'And you came to my aid when it threatened to overwhelm me. You are leaving so soon?'

'It's time, Mr Manike. I need to go home.' Mel almost choked on the words, blinking furiously behind her sunglasses. 'But I'll be writing to you as soon as I get back to London, to find out how you are.'

Mr Manike nodded an acknowledgement. 'May I dissuade you?'

'No. I just need you to get me a speedboat over to Male', by six this evening. I have a flight to Colombo at eight.'

'Without Dr Davenport?' Mr Manike pressed his lips together. 'Dr Murphy, I must tell you that sunglasses are a poor disguise for tears. And that, as manager of this hotel, I would not be doing my job if I did not know where all my guests are sleeping.'

He hadn't even hinted that he knew. Mel supposed that walking around the island holding hands was a pretty sure clue, and imagined that most of the staff and a few of the other guests knew as well. But Mr Manike always seemed so separate from everyone else.

There was no point in the sunglasses any more. Mel took them off and Mr Manike handed her a well-pressed cotton handkerchief from his pocket.

'It's not his fault, Mr Manike.'

'Not yours either, unless I am very much mistaken.'

'No. We're just different. And I don't want to be here for another three days just being angry with him over things that neither of us can change.'

Mr Manike took a deep breath, folding his hands together on the table. 'Dr Murphy, I owe you a great debt. You have used what should have been a holiday to take care of others here, including myself.'

Mel smiled. 'Yes, I'm going to be checking on

whether you take the holiday you promised to. And you owe me nothing. The fact that you're looking much better now is reward enough for me.'

'You are very kind. Mushan will be waiting to escort you to Male' and safely onto your flight, as soon as you are ready. You have a reservation for a hotel in Colombo?'

'I can stay at the airport hotel…' Mr Manike had put two and two together and guessed that she'd be waiting for her scheduled flight home.

'I will arrange your reservation.' Mr Manike opened his desk drawer and drew out a thick card, embellished with the name of a hotel. 'The manager is a personal friend and I will call him now.'

'Thank you…' Maybe this was all getting too real, and the idea that she was leaving Rafe was finally sinking in. Maybe Mr Manike's kindness. Mel wiped the tears from her eyes.

'Dr Murphy. I would like to ask one more thing of you.'

'Of course…'

'Dr Davenport is a good man. Please consider the past, but do not allow it to rule you.'

Rafe had returned to Nadulu and found Mel gone. Hadn't that been exactly what he'd wanted her to do, to go before he had a chance to beg her to stay?

All Mel had asked him for was some kind of plan. He could have stopped all of this and made one with her, but he wouldn't lie to her and he knew she would have seen through his deceit anyway. She knew that he loved her, but that he needed a little time to drill it into his thick skull that love didn't always mean loss.

They'd been blinded, by passion and the belief that somehow they could both change. Maybe they could, but they just hadn't had the time to do it. The best thing he could do now was to face it, and to leave before he hurt her any more than he already had.

All the same, he'd been tempted to take the sea plane and go after her, but it was late in the evening and sea planes were forbidden to fly after dark. Paralysed with fear, that Mel was lost somewhere, in an unfamiliar city and on her own, he went to find Mr Manike. If anyone would know where she'd gone then he would, and maybe Rafe could contact someone who would find Mel and make sure she was safe.

'I understand your concern, Dr Davenport, and admit to having shared it. I had Dr Murphy escorted to her aircraft in Male', and she was picked up at the airport in Colombo and taken to a hotel run by a personal friend of mine. She is there now, and will be escorted onto her flight to London.'

Rafe breathed a sigh of relief. Mr Manike had stepped into the breach and made all the arrangements needed.

'Tell me which hotel, Mr Manike.' He tried to keep his voice level.

'No.' Mr Manike folded his hands on the desk in front of him.

'You mean you don't know?'

'You insinuate that I would allow Dr Murphy to go to an unknown hotel, Dr Davenport?' Mr Manike's tone betrayed his outrage at the thought.

'No…no, of course not. You're not going to tell me though?'

'Dr Murphy asked me not to, and I will not break my word.'

Mel had made the same decision he had. He'd walked away from her, knowing it was the right thing to do, and she'd packed her bags and done her own piece of walking. He took a breath, trying to steady himself.

'Fair enough. You've acted in Mel's best interests and I'm grateful to you for that. I'm sorry you had to get mixed up in this…'

'It has been a matter of some regret to me too. I did offer one thought…'

Rafe didn't want to hear it. There was nothing that anyone could say which would make this any easier. He needed time before he risked believing in a plan for their future together and Mel couldn't give it to him. It was as simple as that.

'That's between you and Dr Murphy too. Will you do me a favour, my friend?'

'Of course.'

'You shouldn't be in your office this late. Shall I see if I can find another pair for a rubber of bridge before you turn in for the night?'

Mr Manike beamed suddenly. 'I think we might both benefit from that. I will order a nightcap…'

Mel had been back in England for three weeks. She wasn't exactly sure, but her impression was that not one day had passed without rain.

Not warm rain. Not heavy rain. The kind that soaked insidiously into your jacket, and trickled icy fingers down your neck. The kind that suited her mood completely, because without Rafe everything was grey and cold.

Ash was a problem. Mel had promised to call him and she didn't want to let him down, but she didn't want to put Ash in a difficult position either.

Maddie came up with the answer.

'I'll get in touch with him. I'll say you're out of town, and that you've passed his number on to me. I might even be a bit more use to him than you are. He wants to specialise in surgery, you say?'

'Yes, you're a lot more relevant to what he wants to do than I am. Do you mind?'

'No. I mind that you won't call his father.'

'We're done, Maddie. Rafe's a great guy but we're not compatible. I made the right decision.'

'Which is why you're so happy about it.'

Mel stared miserably at the table between them. Maybe she shouldn't have suggested this coffee shop. The music was making her want to cry.

'Why does this place always have to play these...songs?'

'You never minded it before.' Maddie took a sip of her cappuccino. 'And that's a case in point, Mel. If you can't stand an ever so slightly sad song about love, then that says it all. Trust me, I know these things.'

'Maybe I should call Rafe. Just apologise to him and end things properly.'

Maddie rolled her eyes. 'No! If what you want

is to end things, then it's already done. Finished. You either let it go or you call him and tell him you want to start things up again. Apologise if you like. I don't think that matters one way or another.'

'It matters. I just walked away.'

'If someone had asked me to give up my job and go on a three-month jaunt around Sri Lanka I'd have thought twice about it as well.'

'He didn't exactly say that.' Mr Manike's words echoed in Mel's head. Consider the past but don't allow it to rule you.

Maddie puffed out a sigh. 'Okay, well, you know what I'd do?'

'No.'

'You're trying to find a way to end well, and there isn't one. Accept that you're not done with the guy yet, and decide where you want to go from there.'

Rafe arrived back from Nadulu, slinging his bag down in the hall. Everything was going well in that part of the world. Everything seemed to be going well back in Colombo. There were no messages for him at the hospital, no requests for urgent medical help. He slumped down onto the sofa. Everything was going so well that he just might drown his sorrows and get very drunk tonight.

His phone rang, and he answered it. *Please* let this be someone who needed his urgent and single-minded attention. Someone who would stop him feeling the grief over losing Mel.

'Rafe Davenport.'

'Hello…?'

The caller didn't need to introduce herself. He knew exactly who it was. Rafe sprang to his feet.

'It's Mel.'

'Mel. How are you?'

'Good. You?'

'Yes, I'm good too.'

Silence. Was this what Mel had called for? Had she hung up? Terror at the thought made him blurt something—anything out.

'Mr Manike's well.'

'Ah, good. He's been getting some rest, has he?'

'Yes, and he's spoken to the owners of the hotel and told them he needs an assistant. They agreed immediately. They know that he runs the place like clockwork. He's far too valuable to them to lose.'

Three whole sentences. Rafe congratulated himself.

'That's great. I got an email from him the other day, and he said that he'd been well.'

So Mel wasn't phoning about Mr Manike. Rafe searched his mind for something else to say.

'Ash got a very nice message from your friend Maddie the other day.'

'Ah, good. He didn't mind me passing his number on?'

'No, he's grateful for her help. I appreciate her time.'

'She's more than pleased to do it.'

Another silence. Rafe decided to wait this time, to see if Mel would say something.

'I'm glad you're well, Rafe.'

'Thanks. I'm very happy to hear that you're well.'

'I'll…um… I'd better let you go.'

'Yes…' Rafe grimaced. He hadn't meant that. He'd meant, *No, don't go, because I need to talk to you.*

'Right, then. I'll… Nice to speak to you, Rafe.'

The line went dead. Rafe stared at his phone. 'Hello…? Mel…?'

What was that all about? Suddenly Rafe knew exactly what it was about. Mr Manike hadn't been the only person at the hotel who had wondered aloud whether Rafe would like to talk. Ash had made a point of taking him for lunch when he'd arrived back at the hospital and talked.

Mel had friends. Maddie must know what had happened, and in Rafe's experience that meant talking. Everyone had been talking apart from the two people who really needed to talk, because they'd broken each other's hearts.

And that was going to have to change. Right now.

CHAPTER SIXTEEN

RAIN. AGAIN. IT had been almost two days since Mel had called Rafe, and all she'd been able to think about was how she'd made things worse. She hadn't ended well, or opened a line of communication. She didn't even have the consolation of having said what she wanted to say.

Maybe she should call again. Maybe she should just let it alone. There must be a third option because the first hadn't worked so well and the second was utterly impossible.

The doorbell was a welcome diversion. It would take at least a minute to take a parcel in for next door, and that would be one minute that she wasn't thinking about Rafe and wondering what to do next. Only when she answered the door it appeared that finally stress had got the better of her, and she was now hallucinating.

'Mel.'

'Rafe.' That was all Mel could think of to say.

'Mel, you were right and I was wrong. I

walked away when you needed me the most, and I let you think that I didn't care enough to work things out. But I love you, and I'll go down on my bended knees and ask you to forgive me, and to marry me. And…live with me, wherever you want to live. Have sex with me whenever you're so inclined.'

Mel stared at him. Clearly he hadn't planned what he wanted to say to her. He'd just been the Rafe that she was irreversibly in love with and gone with the flow.

'Do you want to come in first?'

He looked around at the wet garden and dropped his holdall on a dry spot in the porch. 'I could do it here…'

'Rafe! This is England, not a tropical island. People don't just fall to their knees proposing all over the place.' She reached forward, grabbing the front of his jacket and pulling him inside. Rafe staggered over the step and into the hall, managing to catch up the handles of his bag as he went.

'Here, then.'

'You're serious?' Bright warmth had suddenly flooded into Mel's world, and she wanted nothing more than to feel Rafe's arms around her.

He held his hands out in front of him. They were shaking. 'Mel, I've never been any more serious about anything. When you called me

I knew that it wasn't over between us. And I knew that we had to stop talking to other people, and talk to each other.'

'In that case...' Rafe was clearly in a bad way over this and there was only one thing to be done. Only one thing she wanted to do. Mel stood on her toes, wrapping her arms around his neck and kissing him.

'Mel...stop.' His whole body was shaking, but he kissed her with the same hunger that he'd always shown. 'You deserve an explanation.'

'I know what happened, Rafe. We loved each other and it just became too hard to bear. It was too much for us to realise that this was something different and that it wouldn't end the way everything else has for us.'

He nodded. 'That's fair. But I was the one who acted badly.'

'We both acted badly. And now we're going to repair that. Because, for the first time in our lives, we're in a place where we can.'

He was staring at her, obviously considering what to do next. Mel knew. It was what she always should have done next. She pulled off his jacket, hanging it on a peg in the hall. Underneath he was wearing a thick sweater and a shirt. Maybe a T-shirt underneath that. Layers of clothes were a new experience and for a moment she savoured the thought.

She started to back up the stairs. 'Rafe, if I get to the top and you haven't got me in your arms, I'm going to order you out of this house...'

Suddenly he was all motion and action. The man she loved, sweeping her off her feet and carrying her upstairs. He made a lucky guess that her bedroom was the one at the front of the house and nudged the door open with his foot.

'Nice bedroom...' He pinned her against the wall, kissing her.

'Clothes, Rafe. Get your clothes *off.* You can admire the decorations later.'

Making love with Rafe was never going to be a hurried affair. It was almost dark by the time they'd got out of bed, and Mel led him downstairs and into the sitting room. She left him looking at the titles on her bookshelves while she went into the kitchen to fetch a bottle of champagne that had been sitting at the back of the refrigerator for months.

He grinned when he saw the bottle and two glasses, wresting the cork from the champagne with practised ease. 'Before we have too much of this, there are some things we need to discuss.'

That was okay now. They were both ready to move forward and make a life together. Mel sat down on the sofa and when Rafe joined her she tipped her glass against his.

'Here's to finding the right path, then.'

He nodded, taking a sip from his glass. 'You have a lovely home, Mel. You have a great career and a life. I understand that you've worked hard for that, and for your peace of mind, and I never want to take that from you.'

'If I couldn't leave then it would turn into a prison, however comfortable it is.'

He kissed her forehead. 'Being able to leave it all behind isn't a reason to actually do it, Mel. Why don't I start with my plan, and then we'll negotiate?'

'Okay. Sounds fair.'

'I want you to marry me. We can keep the house in Sri Lanka on for the time being, because it would be great to be able to go and visit Ash from time to time, but I'll give up my job in Colombo and find one here. We'll be together, and we can either stay in this house or get another one between us. Whatever you want.'

'Hmm.' Mel pursed her lips. 'I like the being together part, very much.'

'That's a good start...' His eyes flickered with humour. 'And the rest?'

'I see us spending the winter in Sri Lanka. Then coming back here to London for the summer. You can show me all of the things you love about Sri Lanka, and I'll reacquaint you with all of the things you used to love about London.'

Rafe thought for a moment. 'I can organise a six-month break from work if you can. And I'm sure there's plenty to keep someone of your expertise busy in Colombo if that's what you want.'

'Likewise, London needs your talents too. So that's settled?'

'Yeah, it's a really good plan. Where would you like to get married?'

'I'm…thinking we won't get married. Not just yet, anyway.'

He stared at her. 'Okay, I'll be honest with you. That's a disappointment. May I ask why?'

'It's not that I don't want to marry you, Rafe. I just want a little time for us to live with our promises. I love you, and I trust you. That means that I can walk away from the past, and my anxiety about the future. I want to show both of us that I can.'

He nodded. 'I think I understand that. In that case, I'll promise you right now that I will love you the way you should be loved, and that I won't leave you. You have my word, and everything that I am, on that.'

'I promise you too, Rafe. I'm going to love you well, and I'm not going to leave you.' She flung her arms around his neck, kissing him. 'I'm so happy. You've made me so happy...'

'May I ask one more thing of you?'

'Yes, of course.'

He got to his feet, walking out into the hallway and feeling in an inside pocket of his jacket. When he returned, sitting down next to her on the sofa, he slipped a ring box into her hand, curling his own hands around hers.

'I know you don't want to get married right now. I respect that, and I think we both need some time to understand that the promises we've made are real and lasting. But will you take this, as a symbol of those promises? You don't have to wear it, just keep it safe...'

'I'd like to wear it.' Rafe's sudden smile told her that he'd like that too.

He took the ring from its box. A clear blue sapphire mounted on a plain band. The stone needed nothing else in the way of adornment, and when he slipped it onto her finger it flashed in the lamplight. Mel caught her breath.

'Rafe! It's beautiful. Whenever did you get the time to buy this?'

He pressed his lips together, looking almost apologetic. 'On the way to the airport. I'd been trying to live without you, telling myself that it was best for both of us, and then you called. I knew I had to come and...'

Mel was laughing now. 'So you dropped everything and went to the airport, buying a ring on the way?' It was the nicest thing he could have done. So like Rafe, and his love of movement and action.

'Almost. I called the hospital first to tell them I was going to England on an urgent personal matter. And I know a little jewellery shop where I was bound to get something nice, which does just happen to be on the way to the airport—' He fell silent as Mel laid her finger across his lips.

'Stop. I love that you decided to come and just did it. And I love the ring as well. It's perfect.'

'I'll make an effort to plan things a little more in the future.' He smiled down at her.

'Don't. Please don't change, because you're the man that I'll always love, just as you are. The one I'm *going* to marry.'

He picked up the two champagne glasses, handing Mel's to her. 'Take all the time you want to think about it. Because persuading you is going to be my greatest pleasure.'

They'd spent six months in Sri Lanka, living in Rafe's house in the hills and working out of the hospital in Colombo, travelling together to the parts of the island where they were most needed. Rafe had been proud of Mel's determination to make the most of her stay, and his adopted country had given her so much in return. Then six months in London. He'd forgotten how much he loved London in the summertime, and Rafe had rediscovered the pleasures of living in the city where he was born. Ash had been staying with them for the last three weeks, and Mel had introduced him to several very senior surgeons from her contacts list, who had been pleased to chat with a young doctor about ways he could pursue his ambitions.

He and Mel had kept their promises. They'd loved each other sincerely and completely, a love that had grown deeper every day. And then Mel had said the one word that had made them consult the map again.

Yes.

It appeared that getting married was far more complicated than just finding a presentable suit, a fabulous dress and someone to marry them. In the end, as they were drinking coffee on the patio after a leisurely Sunday lunch with Ash, Amy and her husband Ben, the matter came to a head.

'We're staging an intervention.' Amy had clearly been elected to speak for all three of them.

'Really?' Rafe suppressed a smile as Mel made a very good job of feigning surprise.

'Yes, really, Mum. You and Rafe are going to make a decision about your wedding.'

'Ah. Well, now you mention it, we really should come to some decision, shouldn't we, Rafe? Let's hear it then, darling.'

'I've canvassed your friends...' Mel's eyebrows shot up at the thought, and Amy started again. 'Actually, I just called Maddie, and she said she'd love an excuse for a holiday in Sri Lanka and she was sure a few other people would as well.'

'But what about Gramps and Grandma?'

'We talked about it when I took Ash round to see them the other day. They say they're up for it, and Ash says that they'll have no shortage of invitations for trips out from the family.'

Mel looked up at Rafe and he nodded.

'No shortage at all. But we're not getting married without you three.'

'Well, then, that's perfect, because Ben and I would really like to go to Sri Lanka and I'm dying to see your house there after all of those gorgeous photos that Mum brought back. Ash says he'll show us around while you're off on your honeymoon.'

'Yes, I'll take them to Kandy, and the rock fortress at Sigiriya. Maybe Yala National Park,' Ash broke in. 'As long as you don't have any of those places in mind. We wouldn't want to crowd you.'

'That all sounds lovely. What do you think, Rafe?' Mel nudged him in the ribs.

'They seem to have everything covered. The guest house is plenty big enough for your parents along with Amy and Ben, and we can put everyone else up in the house. Have the reception in the garden, maybe put up a tent.'

'A marquee.' Ash clarified the arrangement for Amy and Ben's sake. 'It's a very big garden.'

'So what do you say?' Amy beamed triumphantly, and Rafe shot Mel a grin.

'Well, if Mel's happy with the idea I certainly am. Thanks for the intervention, guys. That was really helpful.'

Rafe put the coffee cups into the sink and turned to put his arms around Mel. 'Looks as if we're going to Sri Lanka, then.'

'So it does. Only Amy forgot Mr Manike.'

'That's okay. I'll give him a call tomorrow, and ask him to come across for the wedding. Well done, darling.'

Mel laughed. 'I knew that Amy wouldn't be able to resist stepping in if I told her we just couldn't make a decision. It makes everything so much easier if they think it's their idea.'

'What's next then? After the honeymoon.'

'We've both got a few job offers, here and in Sri Lanka. What do you say we just go with the flow and see where life leads us?'

Rafe kissed her. 'That sounds like a great plan. We'll do that.'

* * * * *

If you enjoyed this story, check out these other great reads from Annie Claydon

From the Night Shift to Forever
Risking It All for a Second Chance
The Doctor's Reunion to Remember
Falling for the Brooding Doc

All available now!